AF397846

Kaya is a sophomore in High School who is just trying to find a way back to her old life. None of her friends or classmates suspect the real reason for her absence over the past few months; the reasons why every day is a struggle and why the last thing she wants to do is let someone get close to her. But when a new student enters her life the darkness that constantly surrounds her begins to shift. Suddenly Kaya finds herself being torn between her darkest urges and the need to share her story. Could Tim be the key to her old self?

Andrina V. Reynolds

When Nothing's Right

Edition 381/www.manuskript-oase.ch

Manufactured in Germany (Books on Demand GmbH, Norderstedt)
First Edition: Autumn 2013
Design by Laila Defelice
ISBN 978-3-9524044-7-8

To Vicky – I love you, Sis

Prologue

Death is easy, peaceful even. Life is just so much harder. With this in mind, I took a deep breath and dragged the blade across my wrist in one swift movement, watching the blood flow out, seeing it drip down my arm and slowly form a puddle on the black and white tiled kitchen floor. I turned on the water faucet and held my arm under the burning stream of hot water. Ignoring the pain, just focusing on what was ahead: relief, escape, the end.

1

I stifle a sigh as I let the memory wash over me like the waves at the beach do whenever I'm too late to dive under them into safety. Of course I'd known the feeling long before that, but nothing compared to the disappointment I felt when I woke up hours later in a bright, sterilized hospital room, a thick white bandage around my wrist; my last memory being the excruciating pain accompanied by the unbearable longing and satisfaction of feeling something; of feeling anything.

As clearly as if it happened yesterday, I can still see my weeping mother sitting in a chair beside my bed. I cringe slightly at the image of her; her tear-streaked face with those big brown eyes, so similar to mine, filled with sorrow and puzzlement at what her only daughter had done, something she would have never expected, much less wanted. She had appeared so small to me and I'd felt the intense need to comfort her, but my father's arms had reached her first. Never will the accusation in his eyes completely fade from my memory. I had never seen him look so old. It was as if he had aged by a decade between the time I was alive and the time I simply wished I wasn't.

"Don't bite." My mum reaches over to touch my arm, but I shy back instinctively, releasing my lower lip from between my teeth. For a second our eyes meet, but I lower my gaze because I can't stand all that is so clearly visible. All the things she is thinking, but she can't say, displayed in her eyes for me to read. Her hands around the wheel tense for just a moment, but I can't bring myself to feel sorry for turning her down. I hear her sigh quietly as she turns her attention back to the road. I wonder briefly what's going through her mind. I even consider asking her, but to be honest, I don't care enough and I don't think I want to know anyway. Why pile even more blame onto myself?

I look out the window, trying to distract myself before I take even more steps down that memory lane, which will inevitably have me crashing down. And I definitely don't need that to happen now, or ever for that matter.

I watch as we drive down these so familiar streets and immediately I get a strange feeling of comfort mixed with a nervous anxiety. The closer we get to our destination, the more I internally brace myself for this next "milestone in my recovery" as Theresa calls it. I still prefer the more common term: school.

I'm actually almost looking forward to it. It is surely going to be more bearable than the constant worried stares of my parents as they watch my every move while I'm at home; or anywhere actually, as they basically haven't left my side since that dark day when everything changed while amazingly staying the same. I'm also nervous though, despite attending the same school for the past three years. Well, more like two and a half if you take into consideration those past months during which I was absent due to my "personal issues", another one of Theresa's favorite terms. And now I'm back for my sophomore year.

"Honey, are you absolutely sure you want to do this?" My mum's voice breaks through the silence, weak, but pleading nevertheless. My jaw clenches and I try not to grind my teeth as she would probably just interpret that as a sign of her being right.

"We don't want to rush anything. Maybe you should stay at home for a little while longer, you know, just until …", I interrupt her, sick and tired of hearing it for the millionth time. Sick and tired of hearing it at all.

"Mum, we've been through this. I want to go back. Now will you please just let me get out?" My hand's already on the door handle, waiting for the first opportunity to finally step back into some sort of normality, to finally escape her 24/7 surveillance.

"Of course, once I find a parking spot. I would prefer not to get a ticket." My hand goes limp, sliding down into my lap. I have to close my eyes, but that only muffles my explosion rather than averting it.

"Mum! You don't have to park! Just let me get out, and I'll see you after school, ok?" I look at her, an angry edge to both my voice and stare. She studies me for a moment, clearly surprised and taken aback by my strong reaction and I watch her eyes wander to my wrist for just a second before flitting back to my face. I don't know what she reads in it that soon makes her exhale, before leaning in to kiss my cheek, but—seeing my expression—she settles on a small wave and a cheerful "have fun!". But no matter how hard she tries to appear unconcerned as I get out of the car as fast as possible, I still feel her eyes on my back until the heavy school doors swing shut behind me.

"Oh my gosh, Kaya!" I hear the squealing voice before I see the face to go with it, though I would have recognized it anytime, anywhere. Doesn't mean the happiness it contains reflects my feelings. I take a deep breath before plastering a huge smile on my face and turning around to face the person I've been hanging out with since the very first day of Junior High. A friend I used to confide in, telling her all my secrets while learning about hers. She's the one friend who could probably name every single crush I've had in the past three years or make a list of all the things that bothered me and she helped me get through. She knows me inside out and yet she only knows the stories, the lies, just like everybody else.

"Hailey!" The words are out of my mouth just a nanosecond before she throws her skinny arms around my neck. My breath catches in my throat with the sudden closeness. I'm glad she can't see my face because I doubt it's as happy as she'd expect it to be. In an attempt to act normal, I hug her back, swallowing the claustrophobia that's slowly rising in my chest.

"Ugh, uhm, love you, but you're suffocating me", I gasp, relieved when she lets go and instead holds me at arm's length, studying me intently.

"Oh my gosh, your hair!" Judging by her incredulous expression I can tell that she hasn't quite decided whether or not she likes it.

"Ok, no need to be all touchy-touchy; it's still my hair, not a wig or something." I swat her hand away and take a small step back.

"Sorry, but it's just so …" She waves her hands frantically in search of a description.

"Brown?" I suggest. She nods like one of those hula-girl puppets you put on the dashboard of your car.

"Why?!" The question I was afraid of. Well, one of them.

"Felt like it. Plus, dark just fits better to Europe." Her eyes light up and I fear the worst.

"Speaking of, how was it? I still cannot believe you ditched all of us to spend some 'quality time' with your aunt in Switzerland! I mean, no offense, they've got great chocolate and that weird sticky cheese dish is absolutely delicious, but still: Switzerland?! I sure could think of more interesting places than that." I grit my teeth, trying hard to keep the smile on my face. Another question I feared.

"It was great. I loved it, nice seeing my family. But of course I missed you so much." My voice sounds flat, even to my own ears, but either Hailey doesn't hear it or just chooses to ignore it because just then she pulls me in for another heart-felt hug.

"Awww! I missed you too!!! Soooo much! Don't ever just skip out on me ever again like that, promise?" I nod mechanically. I do mean it, I don't want to leave her again, but it wasn't like I planned it the first time around. It just happened. But wait: wrong train. Not the way I am supposed to think. It was a one-time thing, something that greatly impacted my life, but an experience that made me wiser and grow as a person; that's the way I'm supposed to see it, according to Theresa. Well, sometimes that can be very difficult. Or even impossible, depends on how you look at it.

Hailey loops her arm through mine and continues chatting away as we make our way to the school office to pick up our schedules. Occasionally she asks me a question, but—by simply nodding and saying "totally" or "no way" from time to time—she does not even notice how distracted I am or how much effort it takes not to push her away and walk straight out of the front door; away from the closeness, the touching, the people and all the damn questions.

When she finally has to let go of me to head down the stairs to the chemistry labs, I can't help but lean against the wall to breathe a sigh of relief as soon as she is out of sight. With a moment to myself, I suddenly realize that this is definitely not how I pictured our reunion to be. And with a pang of guilt I also realize that I never actually did picture our reunion.

"People, you all need to let me breathe!" I exclaim, partly because it's true and partly because group hugs are even worse than one-on-ones. And this is my third today though I only just walked into second period.

They laughingly let me go, but still all three of them huddle close. Their eager happy faces are glowing and my ears are filled with their joyful shrieks and more than annoying questions. I answer each of them, though I try my best to be as unenthusiastic as I can, hoping it will discourage them and that a new topic will be found.

I continue describing how it was, being home schooled by my aunt (though in reality it was my mum and not even remotely close to being as much fun as I'm making them believe it was), while I close my eyes and take a deep breath. I can smell the heavy scent of Katy's signature perfume, Angel. I also inhale a whiff of the typical Clara scent, a mixture between the body lotion and the fragrance she swears by. Throw traces of Emily's strawberry shampoo into the mix and you've got the reason for me taking a step back away from my friends and the overwhelming air. Hurt and confusion cloud their faces. Something inside of me wants to laugh it off, pretend nothing is wrong; then again, if these past months have taught me anything, then it is better to admit when something is wrong than to ignore it until one day you just can't anymore. Until one day your fractured shell breaks, along with your heart, soul and faith.

"Anyway, uhm, enough about me; how were your summers?" The question has an almost miraculous impact because all three of them immediately start chattering. I really try hard to concentrate, but no matter how hard I try, I just can't make myself care. Something is nagging at my mind. Though I'm very glad about the focus shifting from me to them, it did happen pretty fast. Obviously most of us—clearly excluding me—love to share their vacation experiences with others. Especially after summer, when so much always happens. But still; isn't it a little extreme just how fast they went from wanting to know all about my past few months in Switzerland—as if!—to reliving the peaks of their summers?

Gosh, I'm making myself totally crazy again. Overreacting seems to be my specialty lately. They are my friends; they know me well. This is good because their swift subject change just demonstrates how well they can read me. They know that I was feeling uncomfortable with their questions, so they stopped. Perfectly normal, perfectly reassuring. Then why can't I let it go and stop inspecting the situation from every angle as soon as the teacher enters and asks us to settle down?

2

The next few lessons go by in the same manner; friends and classmates questioning me about my absence, while I'm trying to smile through it all. By the time Hailey and I are walking towards the cafeteria for lunch, my cheeks hurt from smiling. I'm really starting to feel great respect for all those celebrities who have to spend days and days smiling through every mean comment, posing for every camera, hiding every secret from the rest of the world.

"… and the buffet! I swear, I must have gained like five Kilos just looking at it; it was so insane. They had those delicious little tarts with lots of …" I hardly even pretend to listen to her, as we push through the glass doors of the cafeteria. The place is buzzing as usual. For a moment I hold my breath, afraid of all heads turning to me. True, up until now no one has seemed even remotely suspicious of my whereabouts these past few months, but what if that changes? What if it is all just some big fat lie, one that will be uncovered the moment I step through these doors?

"Earth to Kaya: Are you coming?" Hailey frantically waves her hand in front of my eyes. I breathe a tiny sigh of relief; no heads turning, no whispers. My secret's still safe.

"Sure, sorry, just had a weak moment of sentimentality. It feels good to be back." I grin at her, and surprisingly I really do mean it as we get in line to grab our food. We both choose the salad bar and I marvel at the normality of the situation. No one is watching me or supposedly protecting me by keeping sharp objects away. I especially appreciate the latter as I marvel at the feel of actual silverware in my hands, not some cheap plastic knife that barely cuts ravioli. I absentmindedly trace the shiny blade with my finger as we pay and make our way to an already full table, where we spot our usual clique.

"Oh my gosh, Kaya, I can't believe it!", Ruby exclaims when she pulls me into another perfume hug before pulling me down into the chair next to her. Her smile is as huge as ever. A twinge of familiarity hits me. Even though she beams at me, I don't miss the dark sparks that fill her eyes for a moment. Same old Ruby, same old people. And they are all sitting around, leaning in, talking at once.

The sudden crowdedness and closeness of the table wipes away the positive feelings of just seconds before. I concentrate on my breathing to avoid freaking out; in, hold it, out, in, hold it, out, in, hold it, out …

I'm so focused on not feeling claustrophobic and ignoring all the voices as best I can that I nearly jump out of my seat when a hand playfully slaps my arm.

"Kaya! Gosh, where are you spacing out to again?" I giggle as if I'm embarrassed, but really I could hardly care less. Hailey laughingly shakes her head and points to Mike who is standing behind us. I'd seen and greeted him earlier that day, so I'm not quite sure why she wants to attract my attention to him. Only on second glance do I notice the guy standing next to him. And only now does Ruby's sudden hair flip and lip pursing make sense.

I'm sure I've never seen the guy before, but he has one of those faces you instantly like. He has one of those faces you just want to trust. Too bad as those guys are exactly the ones you usually shouldn't.

"I'm Tim", he introduces himself in a pleasant voice.

"Kaya", I reply, studying him intently. He's handsome, that's for sure. Still, I wouldn't exactly call him hot though he does kind of remind me of one of the models on the Abercrombie shopping bags. His blond hair is a bit tousled and streaked with highlights which don't look fake but rather like the typical Californian highlights I myself used to have. The kind that come from hours spent on the beach or anywhere really where you're exposed to the often hidden, but nevertheless strong Californian sun. His blue eyes are deep set and friendly. He is wearing jeans and a plain white t-shirt and though I can't be sure, it looks like his torso is pretty muscular. As he takes a seat across from me I continue studying him without being too obvious about it. His jawline is rather angular and it gives his whole face a determined expression. He is tanned, which—so he explains—results from spending the summer surfing in Portugal. His nose is almost a little too big for his face but, for some unexplainable reason, that makes him more attractive instead of having the opposite effect. I'm finding myself liking the way he uses his strong hands to illustrate something he is saying, and every now and then he runs his fingers through his hair, but it doesn't seem like some well rehearsed move, rather like a cute nervous gesture. Wow, this bad boy really has the 'I'm new, a bit shy and almost helpless' look down pretty well.

While the others discuss and dissect every single aspect of their vacation with conversations that are basically identical to the ones we have after every summer, I don't say a word and keep myself occupied by watching Tim. I hope he can't tell, I don't want to seem like some crazy stalker, but even though I know that I should stop and actually listen to what everyone is saying, I can't make myself.

Snippets of their sentences break through my trance nevertheless and each and every single one of them makes me grip the edge of my chair just a little bit harder.

Everyone is telling how great their summer was, how they had had an amazing time, how much they had missed each other. They all make it sound like it is all so easy, so simple, so fun. As if every day of the summer was the most amazing of their life, better even than the one before. Even without hearing their full reports on what they had been up to, they still sound false. Their gushing, their high-pitched excited voices … Tuning them out is becoming harder by the second and even the new guy is not enough to keep me from hearing, from gripping my chair, from feeling incredulous.

When did my friends become so extremely shallow? I mean, seriously, everything was perfect, amazing, incredible, and absolutely fantastic? What about the small everyday problems we all deal with? Are they seriously going to insist that their summer was completely flawless, every single second of every single day? If so, then I suppose theirs and mine are worlds apart. As in, my summer belonged to a real person with real problems while theirs apparently took place in some alternate universe where nothing is ever out of place. Or am I the outlandish one here?

"And what was the worst part about it all?" I ask Kate, who is just in the middle of telling us about her stay in England. For a second she seems shaken, confusion crosses her face, then her expression settles on a cheerful smile, the same as everyone has been wearing ever since we sat down.

"Absolutely nothing! The weather was ok, the food was good and it's just such a beautiful country!" I stare at her, not that she even notices. So that's what defines a wonderful time? The weather, the food and the landscape? A wave of heat—anger—washes over me. I ball my hands into fists, my nails digging into my palm, but instead of shying away from the slight pain in my hand, I welcome it, I love it, I hope it intensifies. My mind is racing. Rarely have I ever felt this out of place and to make matters worse, until an hour ago I thought this was the place where I could finally settle back into my old life, find my way back to my old self. Did that old self include these false, disgustingly cheery, fake friends?

Abruptly I push my chair back and get up. I can't take it anymore; the need to get out of here is almost as strong as the urge to scream. So before anyone can stop me I mumble something about having to pick something up in the school office and storm out of the cafeteria. And for the second time today I feel the eyes on me until the door swings shut behind me.

Biting my lip in order to suppress the scream building up in my chest, I lean my head against the cool wall of the bathroom stall. I close my eyes, too exhausted to keep them open. What the hell just happened? I replay the lunch hour in my head, every conversation and moment except the ones including the new guy. After all, I don't really care if he is fake or shallow. At least I'd know from the start, unlike with all my friends whose true character has taken me completely by surprise. Though, actually, now that I think about it, Tim wasn't so shallow. His stories—as far as I was listening— didn't contain so many adjectives, except to describe the waves he surfed. Must be a "guy thing" not to ornament a story to its fullest or fakest in this case.

Gosh, why didn't I notice before? This question just won't leave me alone. It's hammering against my brain, demanding an answer, which I'm too afraid to admit. My heart knows as much as my mind though that it is true. It sadly isn't that they suddenly turned shallow and fake, that would probably be easier to deal with than reality; my friends have always been this way. They haven't changed, but I have. My world used to be as narrow and perfect as theirs but then it came tumbling down around me. Piece by piece, without me noticing the changes at first, until it was too late. Until everything I've known and believed in was lying in shattered ruins around me, and over these past months all I've been doing is trying to clean up that mess. They, on the other hand, still have their world and beliefs. They didn't come crashing down. They are not imprisoned by the disappointment of breathing or by parents, doctors and therapists and all the other people who try to help me by controlling my moods with medications or wanting me to talk about what I feel inside. It's actually pretty ridiculous: they claim to be professionals, but still none of them seems to comprehend that I did what I did because I wasn't feeling anything inside. So how can I talk about that? How could I ever?

A wave of despair washes over me, but I refuse to admit that my mother may have been right and that maybe it really is too early to attend school. Too early to face reality.

Only a bitter taste in my mouth draws my attention to the fact that I'm still biting my lip. Hard, I even drew blood. I really need to calm down, place a smile on my face and walk through the door back to an apparently normal life. Pretend everything's ok. I used to be scarily good at that.

I try to get into character while simultaneously calming my boiling insides by counting backwards from twenty to zero while breathing in through my nose and exhaling through my mouth. I repeat this exercise until my hands stop shaking and the bell signaling the end of lunch breaks though my trance-like state.

I slip into an empty seat just seconds before my biology teacher—an older, very bored looking man—takes center stage at the front of the room, demanding our attention. He stands motionless until all the conver-sations have died down and the only noise comes from people swiveling their chairs towards him. Then he introduces himself with a monotone voice—Mr. Smith; boring name for a boring man—and asks us to tell our lab partner, the person we will be working with until the end of the semester, a little bit about ourselves.

I've been so preoccupied with my friends that I am bare-ly aware of someone sitting next to me. I turn around in my seat only to find myself looking into two deep-set, friendly blue eyes. Tim. From this distance I notice that they have grey sparks in them, making them seem more alive and vivid than I would have suspected at first glance. I have to restrain myself not to lean forward to discover what other colors they hide. Instead I focus on his face as a whole, not just those interesting, unique blue eyes. He smiles at me and it seems so honest and genuine that I can't help but smile back. Just a little. For some strange reason I suddenly forget how much I actually despise this particular class. It just feels good to have someone smile at me whom I'm not lying to. Well, I am if I tell him about Switzerland, but technically he didn't know me at that point so it doesn't really count as a lie. Clean slate. Then I remember my abrupt departure at lunch and my smile fades along with my short-lived interest in Biology.

I close my eyes for a moment; well, the clean slate was nice as long as it lasted. When I look at him again, I force myself to take on a relaxed posture when really all I want to do is to run away as far as possible from this stupid lab desk, this stupid classroom and especially from this stupid new guy who must be thinking the same thing at this very instant. How could he not, considering lunch. Considering that he most likely regards me as some crazy stranger he has to sit next to for a couple of torturous months. I give a short laugh, dry and hard, no joy in it at all. Clean slate, as if. I probably just perfected his mental image of me; the crazy freak he wants to escape from.

But neither of us gets up, so we do as we were told and open up about ourselves to the complete stranger sitting next to us.

It's warm outside and I let the sun shine onto my bare arms while I lean against the school building, waiting for my mum to pull up. I've purposely positioned myself off to the side of the main entrance because I really don't want to talk to anyone coming out of the building. I just want to be alone with my thoughts. They wander to the Biology class and with that, to Tim. He seems nice enough, I have to admit, and he definitely earned some brownie points for not asking about my departure from the cafeteria. He neither brought it up nor hinted at it, very gentlemanlike. Instead we talked about whether or not we had siblings—he has a two year older brother and a six year younger sister—, about our hobbies—he's a guitar playing swimmer—and, inevitably our summer and of course—shocker—he asked about my stay in Switzerland. Apparently Mike had given him a summary of everyone in our clique, mine includ-ing that I had been staying with family in Switz-erland for the past few months.

When Tim asked me about it, I hesitated despite having told the same story several times today. It had just been so deliciously tempting to tell him the truth about my whereabouts during the last semester. To just quit the lies and be honest; to tell him the truth, up front and without warning. After all, Theresa keeps telling me that it's nothing to be ashamed of; it's just something that shaped who I am now. I should embrace and learn from it, not hide it. Well, technically she never told me not to hide it, she just advised me on how I should feel about it.

My mind strays back to Tim and what would have been, had I been honest. I imagine his expression, the way he would look at me, his blue-grey eyes disgusted and incredulous. I can almost see him lean away from me, shooting frantic glances at Mr. Smith's back, already preparing mentally how he'd ask him for another seat. If he knew my true story, he would definitely think I'm insane. Which, granted, maybe I am, though everyone keeps telling me I'm just "more scarred than others" and "in a dark period of my life". Bullshit.

A car honks loudly and I tear myself out of my slightly twisted daydreams and rush down the stairs to meet my mum and a bunch of hidden questions behind her too innocent "How was your day, honey?" and her slightly too cheerful smile.

3

"Tell me about your first day back." I bite my lip, noticing her writing something down in her notebook. It's A4 with a green cover; it reminds me of poison ivy, so it's a perfect fit. Then again, her writing in it is supposedly assisting her in helping me get rid of the poison inside of me, so maybe it's just irony.

I watch her eyes travel to my face. Immediately I stop biting and change my posture to be more comfortable on the soft, beige leather couch I've spent so many hours on. The room is flooded with sunlight and it's color palette is furnished in light as well, probably to avoid depressing the patients. Good luck with that. I look at the floor, fighting the urge to sink my teeth into my lip again. We're both waiting for me to say something, anything. Even if I didn't answer her question and started rambling on about something totally random, she would still nod approvingly while bending over her poison ivy notebook to take some more notes. Or she'd urge me to go on. "And how does that make you feel?" she'd ask.

I take a deep breath, open my mouth and close it again. No sound comes out. Where shall I start? With how I noticed for the first time how fake and shallow my friends really are? With how lying to all of them is eating me up from the inside but the thought of telling them the truth has me gasping for air?

"Nothing special", I finally manage. I look up to meet Theresa's amber eyes. She is studying me intently, trying to decide what I'm really trying to say. She's been working with me long enough to know that that phrase contains so much more information than I'm willing to offer.

I stare right back at her. She slightly raises an eyebrow, but remains silent. It's the same as always. Well, actually, that's not true. Sometimes I do offer the truth immediately. Though those occasions are rare, no matter how much I have learned to trust her. I have learned that once you say something out loud, it's there. True and out, hardly a chance of taking it back, especially here where everything I say is carefully analyzed.

"Fine", I mutter under my breath.

"What did you say?" She leans forward to catch my words as I slowly come around to describing the feelings inside when my friends were telling me about their vacation.

In contrast to my silence just minutes earlier, my sentences come fast and without any breaks. I let go and leave my heart to do the talking, listening to my own words while my fingers restlessly fidget with the bracelets on my wrist.

It is difficult to talk about everything I feel inside because I've been suppressing any kind of emotions for a long time now. At the beginning of our sessions I barely ever said anything. There were days I would not even greet her. But with time Theresa won my trust, partly because I learned that she would never ever betray me by summarizing our conversation for my parents.

As what I am saying becomes more comprehensible, less urgent, my fingers start to rest, only occasionally sliding a bangle up and down my arm. I suddenly feel tired, so extremely exhausted that when I'm done, when I run out of things to say, I close my eyes and lean back letting the familiar sound of her pen scribbling furiously across the page engulf me. The sound of her writing is so loud in the otherwise quiet room that I notice immediately when it stops, aware of the fact that she is watching me.

"Time's up. Anything else you want to share?" When I shake my head she gets up and opens the door for me.

My room used to be my safety zone, my oasis, my personal island in the midst of chaos. Not that my room was very tidy, but metaphorically speaking of course. Now it's none of those things. Not even untidy because the need to keep my hands busy is so immense I can't help but clean up. A rather nice side effect of my mental state in my mum's eyes. The only nice one.

I lie on my bed flicking through Teen Vogue. The glossy pages used to absorb me, fascinate me. I especially loved the feature on whoever was posing on the cover.

Magazines were, even in these past few dark months, a piece of normality; a piece of who I used to be. Now I can't help being annoyed and angry at every picture of every smiling model. They pose and smile, trying to sell something—if not a product, then the good mood they are in. And their perfect bodies are taunting normal girls—every girl really—because which one of us hasn't wished to have those legs or that figure? And to think that it's all photoshopped, that it's all fake and shallow. Just like my friends.

Angrily I toss the magazine aside and close my eyes, listening to the upbeat tunes of Britney Spears' latest record, Femme Fatale. Music is always the thing I turn to, irrespective of whether I'm upset or not. I love listening to music; it's so full of variety and there's something that fits to everyone and every mood. My iPod is an eclectic mix of old and new, slow and fast, happy and sad. I must have spent hundreds of dollars downloading songs on iTunes. But it's worth it because sometimes those three and a half minutes of just focusing on the lyrics, the instruments and the vibe of the song can make all the difference; can push me back to the safe side, where nothing necessarily is ok, but at least bearable.

I turn my head so I can look at the picture on my nightstand. It shows me and some friends, Hailey, Kate and Emily amongst them. The photo is the most up to date one I have, though my hair is still blonde in it. It was taken when we went ice skating in the mall, back in

January. All of our faces are flushed, but we're all smiling. Happy, cheerful grins. Hailey's arm is around me and even I am beaming into the camera as if everything were as great as it seemed, though by that point it was all a lie. Nothing was great and on the inside I was probably crying. One look into my eyes confirms that. They seem oddly dull and stand in contrast to my grin. How come no one but me ever notices?

I turn around and curl up against the wall. I try to make myself as small as possible, like when I was a little kid and I was trying to hide in my parents' bed. Usually this position has a calming effect on me, maybe because it's so familiar. Today, though, I just feel silly and not protected or hidden in any way.

With a sigh I get up, straighten the covers on my bed and start organizing all my pens, highlighters and erasers. I'm focusing so hard on the task at hand that I only notice that I've been biting my lip when a bitter taste fills my mouth and, after I put it to my mouth, my finger comes away with the slightest red streak on it.

4

If I had to pick an adjective to describe the early morning of my second day of school, it would be "distracted".

It started when my alarm clock went off and instead of hitting the snooze button and getting up, I barely even heard the usually annoying sound of my alarm. I just lay in bed for I don't know how long while staring at the ceiling. I was thinking about the stupidest, most random things, but for some reason I couldn't help it. I couldn't help myself considering what color I would paint my room—if I wanted to change it—or to conjure up the memory of what used to hang above my bed when I was a little kid.

When I finally did manage to get dressed and drag myself downstairs, I just sat there absentmindedly nibbling on a piece of toast. Now, thinking about it, I don't even remember if I put peanut butter on it or not. Not that it matters, because I think—I wasn't really listening so it is hard to tell for sure— that my mother scolded me for barely eating anything anyway. Well, scolded is a very loose term these past few months. I could literally smash a vase on the ground and all she would do is politely suggest that I calm down and ask if there was something I wanted to talk about with someone.

I shake my head lightly, still astonished that she didn't slap me or something; it was, after all, one of her favorite and most expensive vases. But I guess that's one positive thing about being classified as a lunatic (or as deeply depressed, as everyone keeps "oh so politely" reminding me)—I can do what I want and no one can or will say anything because I'm not in a "normal" state of mind. Whatever "normal" is, I wish they'd start treating me like it. The reason I took up the habit of breaking things for a while was because nobody punished me. Nobody even reacted properly, which just made me even more angry, which resulted in more china being smashed which ended with me in a fit and my parents being as polite as they were all along. Ugh—just the mere thought of it makes me boil. I hate being treated like that.

Using my annoyance at my parents and their "far from normal" behavior (doctors and therapists are not the only ones who can use such terms freely) as fuel, I round the corner in the hallway a bit faster than I usually would. Clearly with consequences because as soon as I do so, a strong impact sends the book in my hand flying to the floor and me stumbling backwards. I stretch out my arm, trying to steady myself on the wall, just as a helpful hand reaches out to prevent me from falling and making an even bigger fool of myself.

"Thank you", I mumble, double embarrassed for what just happened and because I feel my cheeks turning pink.

I peek up at the person I almost ran over and find myself once again staring into Tim's gripping eyes. Today the grey is barely visible, the blue being even more dominant than yesterday. It is so clear, I feel myself getting lost in them.

"I'm so sorry! Are you ok?" I nod, startled by his voice. Only now do I notice his hand still gripping my arm. I jerk away. Oops, that was probably rude, especially because he just saved me. So I flash him a tiny smile before dropping to my knees.

My books and pens are scattered everywhere and it's not the first time in my school career that I silently curse myself for not carrying a bag. I start picking up my things, reaching around him to grab some pencils. From the corner of my eye I see him do the same.

"Thank you", I say again as he hands me a stack of notebooks, careful—it seems—not to touch me. I must be imagining things.

"You should seriously carry a bag or at least a pencil case—would make running into you a whole lot easier." He winks at me, waves slightly and continues down the hallway as if nothing ever happened. After a couple of steps he turns around again.

"See you in Biology!" he calls and, despite myself, I smile.

Though it is uncharacteristic of me, I'm actually looking forward to Biology. I wouldn't admit it to anyone, but I do feel a kind of excitement when I think of that particular lesson. And that feeling intensifies whenever I remind myself that it most likely has absolutely nothing to do with meiosis or any other kind of cell division we're about to learn about.

It is strange how fast things can change. It was only yesterday that I was planning on running out of the classroom, and now I'm actually anticipating the hour I get to spend in those four walls.

Throughout the whole morning I catch myself discreetly looking up and down hallways. I scan the crowds surrounding me or my locker. Every time I catch my self doing it again, I feel crimson flooding my cheeks though I'm pretty sure no one has noticed my new obsession, and then I try to convince myself that what I'm searching for are simply my friends. I'm good at convincing myself, as well as others. Of course I am, I have a lot of practice. Convincing, smiling, pretending—it was basically all I was doing those last months before everything changed, before everything became even more messed up.

But, despite how much I tell myself that I'm only looking for my friends and that this is a normal reaction to not having seen them in months, deep down I know better. Well, technically I guess I am actually trying to spy a friend, but not just anyone of them. Then again, could he even be considered a friend yet? Will he ever be?

Either way, I honestly cannot pinpoint exactly what it is, but something about Tim fascinates me. Which, considering that I only met him yesterday, could definitely be classified as borderline creepy. But I just can't help it. What's more, crazy people are creepy anyway, so I suppose I'm just doing myself justice.

It's lunchtime and I'm walking into the cafeteria holding my breath. It's ridiculous, really. It's not like his presence or lack thereof would change anything. Not now, not today and not in my life.

I try to keep that thought in my mind, kind of like a mantra, but I completely forget about it when I spot him sitting at the same table as 24 hours before. A smile spreads across my face. The second one today and oddly enough he was the reason for both of them.

I watch him as he laughs at something Mike is saying and then runs his fingers through his hair—which is, like every time I've seen him, a bit messy. Suddenly an overwhelming urge to touch it overcomes me. I'm used to urges; before that day that changed everything I used to "be weak" (Theresa's term, not mine; I just look at it as something I had to do, like breathing) and give in to them, but now I'm learning to resist and to fight them.

So I force my eyes and thoughts away while I buy my salad and walk over to them. Not glancing in his direction is hard, but I manage until I'm confronted with a problem.

There are only three free seats. One is diagonal to Tim, the second one is two seats to his left and the third one is at the other end of the table. I slow my step while I'm approaching, not sure of where to sit. Like a magnet, my gaze travels to his face and his tousled dirty blonde hair.

The other end of the table is definitely too far away and next to that empty seat sits Cecily, a girl I'm not too proud of knowing. So seat number three is out. I hesitate for another moment—just long enough to peak at him again—before sitting down in seat number one, diagonal to Tim. He looks up briefly, flashing me a smile, making my heart almost beat. Almost. Then he reengages in his conversation with Mike and I focus on every bite I take, utterly focused not to look up again until the bell rings, signaling the end of lunch.

"Ready to learn an absolutely fascinating new fact about cell division?" I look up to find Tim standing in front of me. In a moment of low self-esteem I look around, but clearly he must be talking to me. Of course, because right now I'm bathing in the glory of having his magically blue eyes watching me. Taking a deep, but subtle, breath, I get up, trying not to appear too eager.

"Always." He smiles.

I'm rummaging through my locker, making sure that I have everything I need. I already have a pile of books stacked in my arms. Pencils, highlighters and my eraser are balancing on top of them. I completely forgot how much useless stuff a high school student has to constantly carry around. I mean, seriously, it's ridiculous.

"Babe, that looks heavy." I feel a warm hand on my shoulder and spin around, nearly dropping my pile to the floor.

"Woah, careful." Two helpful hands lunge forward and help me steady everything before I make a fool out of myself.

"Thanks, Ruby. You're a lifesaver."

"Oh I know." She grins and winks at me, looking so selfconfident I want to slap her in the face.

"Humble as always." Though she clearly hears my murmur she chooses to ignore it and instead fixes me with her penetrant stare.

"Honey, I just wanted to check in with you. We haven't managed to find a time to talk and catch up yet. I want to hear all about Switzerland. You must have had an amazing time!"

"Uh, ya, totes. We should do that."

"Great. I'll text you, ok? Bye, babe." She blows me a kiss and rushes off, letting her promise linger in the air like an unspoken threat.

"I'll text you, ok?" I know my quiet impersonation of her is terrible, but it makes me feel slightly better about my whole crappy day. Venting is always good. "Let out your emotions. Don't bottle them up." Sometimes I really love Theresa's advice.

Turning back to my locker I focus again on my mental to do list. "Biology, History … uhm … French" I murmur, leaning in deeper and ruffling through my notebooks to find the one I'm looking for. With a triumphant feeling I pull out the blue cahier and add it to the pile in my arms.

"Boo!" a voice says into my ear. With a high pitched shriek I let everything drop. So much for balancing. Seriously, why can't people leave me alone until all my things are safely in my bag? I feel a pang of annoyance for whoever made my stuff end up on the floor for the second time today. Spinning around I see Hailey doubled over with laughter.

"I'm sorry, but I did not see that coming … I was like boo and you were like …" She tries to catch her breath as another wave of giggles hits her.

"Hilarious", I mutter through clenched teeth. Seriously, she should know better. I've always been extremely jumpy; shrieking and dropping stuff included.

"Oh, lighten up!" She drapes her bony arms over my shoulders. Immediately I stiffen. I can't help it, but luckily she does not seem to notice. Weird, she's one of my best friends; shouldn't she realize something is strange about the way I act? Then again, she does believe my story about Switzerland and me claiming that everything is fine and I'm just tired or not feeling well. Something I've been saying for the past year and a half.

"Sorry, just stressed about school I guess." Hailey swivels me around so that I face her. She is squinting at me while pursing her lips. I raise an eyebrow, not quite sure how to interpret her expression.

"Stressed about school? Already? Sweetie, it's the second day!" I'm lacking a smart answer, so I just shrug and hope she'll drop it. She doesn't.

"I've got it!", she suddenly exclaims, clapping her hands in a childishly giddy manner. Oh oh. I know that face and I know that gesture and I know that all it could mean is that she has some "genius" plan. And I also know that they are usually either completely crazy or impossible to execute.

"You need a girls' night! We haven't done that in like forever! Just you, Emily and me. Movies, pizza, nails … and the only guys allowed are Ben & Jerry!" She smiles at me brightly, clearly pleased with her idea. Girls' night; I smile at the memory of dozens of evenings spent just the way she described it. They were always fun, relaxing and exactly what I needed. I loved them; they were our thing.

"I can't, sorry." I'm surprised at my own words and I think about taking them back as soon as I see her face fall. She looks hurt and I swallow emptily.

"Well, it doesn't have to be tonight … this weekend maybe?" I don't want to hurt her anymore, so I do what I've become very good at; I pretend, I act, I lie.

"Uhm, I'm not sure right now but I'll check, ok?" Her smile reappears and she drops to her knees next to me to help me pick up my stuff.

"Thanks." I smile, though it feels more like a grimace.

"So, check for this weekend, ok? It'll be like old times!"

"Just like old times", I agree, while the words make me cringe internally. She leans in to give me a kiss on the cheek; our usual way of saying goodbye.

"Oh and, seriously, clean up your locker!" She winks and disappears into the crowd before I can throw her a look.

5

I lie in bed, trying not to sleep, trying not to stay awake. As so often in these past months, I don't know what I want. I only know what I don't want: this. I roll over, bury my face in my cushion and scream until I'm out of breath. Then I scream some more. It helps but it doesn't release me. It doesn't make the pain go away and it doesn't erase the numbness which is threatening to swallow me. Tears trickle down my face like drops of rain falling onto the ground after a long period of drought. They are welcome, but cause problems nevertheless because earth that is too dry will just end up flooded. I try to wipe them away but they elude me.

I press my face deeper into my now damp pillow. Darkness surrounds me completely. It's the middle of the night; no light is on in my room. My eyes are pressed shut against the fabric. I'm hot and breathing is becoming more difficult. There is a lump in my throat and not even swallowing is an option.

I've never been very religious, but people always have advice on what you need to do in order to go to heaven. What they never tell you is what you should do when your whole life has gone to hell. For the bajillionth time I wonder what I did to deserve this. What I can do to stop this.

I don't know why, I feel this way after a relatively good, normal day. This empty, this hollow, this much in pain. The doctors call it depression, but not me. For me there is only one way of describing it: so damn unnecessary.

Rolling over to give in to my lungs' urge, I breathe. And stare into nothingness. And breathe some more, and stare some more. And it's all I do until I finally drift into a dark, exhausted sleep in the wee hours of the morning.

I wake up, rays of sunlight engulfing me like a warm hug. My tears have dried and the pain subsided enough to let me get up and go about my daily routine. This is more than I was able to do just a few months back.

I hate the way I felt last night; the way I've been feeling for too long. The way I'm fighting to appear normal; the way rarely anything can be considered normal these days.

Walking into the kitchen, I see my mom shooting me a concerned look, a crease forming between her eyebrows. She must have heard my screams, or at least the audible ones. Because the real ones, the ones that come from all the bottomless pain I'm in, those are locked away too deep inside my heart for even me to release. And those are the ones that are eating me up inside, that are breaking me down, that make me feel like I did last night.

I ignore mom and whatever she is thinking. I don't have the strength to deal with her right now, or ever for that matter. All I can do is get ready for school mechan-ically. Trying not to give in takes everything I have. Sometimes holding your head up high can be hard, especially when it feels like the weight of your whole world is pressing down on your shoulders.

When I was a little girl, I used to think I was strong because I was able to beat my friends in arm wrestling, but now I've learned that real strength means keeping it together even when you are falling apart inside. Because if you manage to survive even yourself, then you are strong enough to survive anything.

So, taking a deep breath, I walk out the door ready for whatever fate holds in store for me.

"One week already, wow." She sounds almost honest-ly impressed as if I just told her I had climbed Mount Everest during my summer or something. She definitely chose the wrong profession; she should be working in Hollywood rather than in this light but depressing office in La Jolla. Though I must admit, I'm glad she chose this over L.A. because from all the therapists and doctors I've talked to (or had sessions with, as silence was all they got out of me), she is by far my favorite.

"And how do you like sophomore year so far?" I raise my eyebrows. Just because Theresa has earned my approval, it sadly enough does not spare her nor me from her sometimes silly questions, such as this one. After all, the last time she saw me was three days ago and the first thing she asked then was basically the same, but simply phrased in a different way. And in between that silly question and this one was the weekend. She seems to note my expression and tries a new approach.

"How was your weekend?", she asks. My parents are paying a lot of money for these hours, so I'm glad she is not a dimwit and actually corrects her mistakes to make the most out of both our times. Not that I care about how much my parents spend; they deserve every dollar that is taken off of their accounts.

How was my weekend? I ponder the question for a while, nod slowly, shake my head and then shrug my shoulders. It had been uneventful, made even more so by the text I received from Hailey, wishing me a good time at my grandmother's in Newport. It was a lame excuse but the only one I could think of when she had asked me repeatedly about setting a date for the sleepover.

I debate whether or not to tell Theresa about that night a couple of days ago. I didn't mention it in our last session due to the fact that I was embarrassed; I still am. Sometimes I feel sort of stupid. Others my age have no problem living their lives with the usual minor ups and downs. But me, I come crashing down from high mountain tops into the deepest, darkest valley of an ice cold ocean.

And now I don't know if it is even worth bringing up anymore. It was nothing unusual for me and since that night my life has been relatively stable, with only slight touches or echoes of the things I was feeling inside that night.

Plus, not even Theresa would understand; no one ever does, no matter how much they claim they do. She really would though, a small voice whispers in the back of my mind. Usually I would ignore it, but this time I can't because I know it is right. She really would understand; she really does understand. Not because she has a degree in psychology or because she has probably seen dozens of cases similar to mine, but because she's been there herself. Because she has experienced firsthand what it is like to want something so bad even though you know that the rush of it never lasts and when it wears off, you come crashing down harder than ever. Every single time.

I remember so clearly the day I came in and we sat in silence until I looked up to meet her eyes. It was one of our first sessions; the first one in which she ever heard my voice. I didn't understand what she was doing when, without a word, she rolled up her sleeves, revealing the faint, white lines crisscrossing her arms. They were strangely similar to mine but still very different. Much more openly displayed and seemingly more carelessly done. But no matter how much I may have tried to compare her story to mine, there is and will always be one difference which sets us worlds apart. She, as opposed to me, never took it too far. Just far enough.

Whenever I think of how she has won me over, of what initially made me open up towards her, I feel stronger in telling what is in my heart and this time is no exception.

"Well, my weekend was uneventful, I guess. Which is totally fine, perfectly ok actually. Better than that, compared to … uhm … compared to …" I close my eyes for a moment, crack my knuckles involuntarily, cringe and then, with my eyes still closed, go on.

"… compared to last week. When I felt it again. That horribly sucky feeling. It was in the middle of the night and I don't know why, but I just couldn't suppress it. I couldn't fight it. It was gnawing at me. I screamed into my pillow and I cried but all I really wanted was to …" I break off abruptly and try to swallow, but my mouth has gone dry at the memory. My body tenses and I dig my nails into my palms. A pointed look from Theresa reminds me of a trick she taught me so I spread my fingers and press my hands onto my legs.

"All you wanted was to do what?" I glare at her; she knows exactly what I was going to say but she just widens her eyes innocently.

"You know what", I hiss, but she doesn't seem the least bit affected. Instead she just gestures for me to go on.

"To cut, ok? To take a friggin knife and to cut my skin. There, I said it, happy?" Theresa ignores my question like so often when she knows it would be pointless to answer.

"Why? What would that have helped? It would still be pain, just maybe in a different form." I've heard this argument a thousand times, but it still throws me off guard. It's the one thing that always stands in communications way. People just don't seem to understand what I mean. Though Theresa should. Though Theresa does; but I suppose making me say it is part of her strategy.

"Maybe, but it's not the same." I take a deep breath and continue in a friendlier manner.

"It's different. I can control it. And it's not pain, it's relief. It's something good, something that makes me know I'm alive. It's what keeps me alive. It gives me something to focus on besides the pain inside, besides what's killing me from inside out." My voice drops and she has to lean forward in her big armchair to catch my next words:

"I wanted it so bad. I even imagined it. Imagined what it would feel like when the blade cuts through my skin like it's a piece of soft butter, like there is no resistance. How I'd see a red line slowly form, how the burning sensation would suddenly hit me, but it wouldn't hurt because I did it on purpose. Because now I'd be free. When it happens by accident, then it's uncomfortable and hurts. But not this time. The burning and what some would call pain was anticipated, welcomed. It would be relief from what's slowly but too steadily still killing me from the inside."

"But you didn't. That's what counts. You fought it, no matter how convinced you were that you'd give in. You didn't. But Kaya, tell me, what's slowly killing you?" Her voice is soft. There is no trace of judgment in her eyes; her gaze is calm and inquiring.

I hesitate; we've been trying to get to the bottom of it for several months now and though we've found answers, none of them seems right. I know everyone keeps insisting my hunch is wrong, but there is only one answer that seems even remotely close to the truth.

"I am."

The day goes by slowly and I have trouble focusing on anything. I'm using up all my strength not to snap at my friends, though occasionally I can't help myself lashing out at them. I'm exhausted and beyond annoyed. Smiling around them, even if it's fake, is becoming more and more difficult. If I was hoping their shallowness and fakeness was only a phase, well then I was dead wrong. Every day it seems as if they find a way to top their previous behavior. One day they are gushing about that absolutely dreamy senior, the next about how cute Justin Bieber is and then they move on to finding some overly priced pair of shoes absolutely adorable. Seriously, a guy in our school, fine, I do see the appeal; Justin Bieber? Well, at least he is a breathing human being and considered cute by millions of girls. But a pair of sparkly heels? Completely and utterly ridiculous. And worst of all, until last winter I used to be exactly the same way. Well, not anymore! Things have changed and so have I. No way around it and apparently no way around my friends and me suddenly being farther apart than ever before. Worst of all, they are not even aware of it.

"Careful, gorgeous, or you'll walk into a locker or something." I spin around to look at the person giving me such subtle and sweet compliments. Wow, I never knew Tim was such a liar.

"Nice try, but I'm not so fond of fake compliments. And I am perfectly aware of where I am going, thank you very much." He laughs, a cute dimple forming in his cheek.

"Who says it was fake?", he challenges. My heart flutters a tiny bit at his words. Guess my vital organs have never heard of something called a joke.

I narrow my eyes into slits and purse my lips, trying to look menacing. Apparently though I'm not half as intimidating as I wish to be because he only laughs and gives my waist a playful tug. Immediately his smile fades.

"Sorry", he mumbles almost incomprehensibly.

"What for?" The question seems to make him uncomfortable and he deliberately avoids looking me in the face. I've never seen him like this—though I'm pretty sure there are multiple sides of him which I haven't seen. After all I've only known him for a week and a half, which doesn't exactly pass as an eternity, even though sometimes it feels like one. He cracks his knuckles and

I barely flinch, too intent on wanting to know what he was apologizing for.

"Well, you know, you don't really like to be touched and I just did so well …" I stare at him, stunned. He picked up on that?

"You noticed that?" I ask, the words out of my mouth before I can stop myself. He nods, his eyes checking for my reaction. I try to keep a poker face, but I guess I'm sort of ruining that by biting my lip. So instead, I turn away, letting my hair cover my face like a dark brown curtain.

I feel him watching me while we're walking down the hall to Biology class. I'm too afraid to look at him, too worried about what I might read in his eyes. We are silent the whole way long; each one of us lost in our own thoughts, which are probably entangled in that short, strangely in-depth conversation we had just exchanged.

When we get to the classroom he steps aside gallantly, letting me walk through first. Surprised, I look up into his friendly face; any trace of wariness and of the somber Tim I had seen for the first time a few minutes ago are gone. I smile at him and feel a shiver of happiness when he beams back at me.

6

Despite my newly discovered interest in Biology, it is still not my favorite subject. I love the class because of the people—ok fine, person—in it, but the topics are not what interest me. They seem dull and not seldom do I wonder when I will ever be facing a situation where I will be able to apply this knowledge.

No, it's not my favorite. My favorite subject—the one I absolutely love—is English. I'm good at it, I see the sense in it and I'm interested. Well, the grammar part is not too thrilling, but I get through it. It's worth enduring just to be able to experience my favorite topic—literature.

I adore reading. I do it all the time. I read historical novels, fantasy, romance … the only genres I don't enjoy are thriller, horror and crime. They freak me out and result in many sleepless nights, more than I already have to live with.

What I love so much about reading is that you can escape. Even in the past few months it was one of the only things that didn't change. My passion for it may have even grown. In books, everything is possible. And, unlike movies, you don't have a picture of the characters and the settings so you can use your imagination. One day the heroine of a novel may resemble me, the next she is everything I'd like to be. Books are so diverse; they give you a glimpse of the author's mind. Whether the story is fiction or not is irrelevant. The style reveals so much about the writer. After reading a book, I feel like I know the person who created this work of fiction or who lived through this reality a bit better.

I like movies and I enjoy the cinema very much, but it can never compete with my books. My favorite ones have been read so many times they almost fall apart. There are times when I don't feel well and all I have to do is flick through one of those books, read some underlined passages and I feel better already. True, this magic faded the more I lost the light in my life, but it was there and it is always something I tend to turn to, no matter how minimal its effects might be.

I'm excited when I walk into English on Friday. Friday lessons, Mr. Mason announced, will be dedicated entirely to literature. We'll be reading different books, an eclectic mix of various genres and themes, throughout the year. The first assignment will be done in groups. Each group will read something different, and in a few weeks, presentations will be held. Literature and presentations—two things I like, two things I'm good at.

"Helloooo hellooooo helloooooo", Emily sings. She loves reading and literature almost as much as I do, and she's been telling me how much she is looking forward to these Friday lessons every single day.

"Hey, Em!" I smile cheerfully. Looks like I've still got what it takes to be a good actress, though for once it's not all pretense. The smile isn't my immediate reaction, but forcing it goes smoothly and I almost convince myself that everything is ok. Almost.

"Sit next to me; I already reserved us some seats." She waves me over to two desks at the window. I smile so brightly I'm surprised my face does not crack, and slide into the seat next to her.

"Oh my gosh, I love your top!" She is referring to my black tube top with several silver chains dangling from it.

"Thank you." And I really do mean it. For a while, I used to be very criticized by my friends for what I wore. They'd make jokes about me looking gothic or slutty. True, they were only kidding, but there were moments when the line between joke and opinion was more blurry than ever. Those comments hurt me though I tried my best no to show it, and I lost my confidence in how I dressed. Granted, I'm not the type to follow the latest fashion trends nor am I one of those preppy girls. My style is a little edgier than my friends', but I do have pieces that even they would wear.

"I'm so excited! I wonder what books we'll be reading. What do you think? Wuthering Heights, Jane Eyre and Emma? Or maybe Twilight, I Am Number Four and Stormbreaker? Or maybe …" I clasp my hand over her mouth before she can continue. Immediately I jerk it away.

"Ew! You could have warned me about the gloss!" I wipe my hand on the table in a weak attempt to get the sticky, glossy stuff off my hand. Emily smirks, trying not to laugh and failing miserably.

"Will teach you not to put your dirty hand over other people's mouths!" I roll my eyes and sink back into my chair. Acting like before—or normal, as some call it—can be exhausting.

"Well, I didn't know what else to do to shut you up. Just chill it—we'll know soon enough." As if coordinated, at that moment Mr. Mason enters the classroom in the same focused, swift step with which he moves everywhere.

"Hello class, please take a seat." He places his brown leather folder on the desk at the front of the room. Then he turns to two strong, almost square guys in the first row.

"Could both of you gentleman please assist me in carrying the book boxes?" They get up and the three of them leave the room. Minutes later they return, each carrying a big—by the looks of it heavy—box full of books.

I feel excitement building inside of me. I love new books; the smell, the feel of them, the story they're hiding.

"Thanks gentlemen. Ok class, as you know I've put you into groups already, so I'll pass out the books you'll be reading. Look at them, study them a little and then get into your four groups to discuss your first impressions. Any questions?" Everyone shakes their head. Mr. Mason looks around the class, then starts handing out the books according to the list he is carefully checking.

Some groans are audible, but most just smile and dive into the blurb of the novel they'll be spending many nights with.

I try to peek at what the others are getting, but it's hard to see. The only title I can catch is "Clean" by Amy Reed. I'm familiar with that one. It's about a group of drug addicts in rehab. I wonder what all the books may have in common. I'm convinced that as soon as I get mine, I'll have more insight.

Mr. Mason has finally reached my row. He is getting closer with every book that is being received by one lucky student. Soon it's me.

He stops next to me, checks his list and then slides a book out from under the stack in his arms. I briefly smile up at him as he hands it to me. With a wide, honest grin I focus on what is in my hands. My eyes zoom in on the cover and my breath catches in my throat. The paperback suddenly feels heavy and the room gets hot. I feel myself breaking out into a sweat. I try to swallow, but my throat is parched. The smile vanishes from my face and I have to close my eyes for a moment. The book slides out of my hands and falls to the floor. A few heads turn towards me, but I barely notice. I'm steadying myself on my desk, holding on to the edge. Nausea overcomes me and I have to fight the urge to scream at the top of my lungs. I can hear Emily talking to me, but I can't comprehend her words.

I'm battling memories which come so fast that as soon as I manage to suppress one, another is already waiting to swallow me.

A dark night in my room, all by myself. A bright afternoon when I was home alone. My room, the bathroom, the living room, the library, the kitchen. The memories and images spin faster and faster until I seriously believe that I'm going to throw up. And all of it is accompanied by words which float through my mind and heart like a mantra I can't escape from. It's a poem, so clear I feel as if someone is whispering it into my ear.

It involved a blade
And a soul that's lost
Into the dark she would fade
And blood was all it cost

And suddenly it all stops. The spinning, the whispering, the remembering. It all stops at one image, right there in front of me. With shaking hands I pick up the book, the one image as clear as cut ice. The cover is black with reds lines crisscrossing everywhere. And in the center of it all, in blood red, is the title: Cut.

7

"It's probably a pretty dark story." The boy who just spoke puts the obvious in such a neutral way that it stands in great contrast to what the girls in my group are expressing.

"Dark? More like disgusting! Only disturbed people would do that." Ha—there we have it. I'm not the only one who puts my "darker times" that way. A smile creeps across my face. This is going to be interesting.

"Don't judge! They all have their own—most likely twisted—but nevertheless own story. Those people just can't handle it." That's one way to look at it. I'm starting to like that dude, John I think. He does have a good point. Then again, is that the reason? Because I couldn't handle my perfect life? I couldn't stand being happy, so I had to go and ruin it? Hm, maybe he isn't so smart after all.

"And we all know where that 'own story' will end", she—Angela I believe—puts in her five cents, "in the grave. Because that's exactly what all these sick, attention-seeking people are aiming for. They want to die. At first it's just self harming—something described as an illness—and then they take it too far, just slitting open their wrists or something and then that's that." I glare at Angela; she has fiery red hair, though—to match the rest of her girly appearance—blonde would be more fitting. I barely know her, but I definitely don't like her. She has nothing open minded about herself. True, what she said hits rather close to home, but still. It's callous to judge, especially in that tone.

Suddenly I'm aware of three pairs of eyes on me. I'm the only one who hasn't contributed anything. What do they want to hear? I'm for sure not going to agree with Angela, no matter how right she might be in some cases, nor do I want to support the other girl's shallow opinion (what was her name again?), and I don't feel like underscoring John's opinion either.

"To kill yourself you'd have to cut lengthwise, not across." The words tumble out of my mouth before I'm aware of them being on my mind.

The nameless girl pales and pulls her face into a grimace of revolt, while the guy just studies me with a scrutinizing gaze. Angela, on the other hand, puts into words what they are thinking.

"Why the hell do you know that?!" I blink, trying to come up with a fitting answer.

"I … uhm … I read an article?" The statement was meant to come out all confident and strong. It was meant to put a stop to any further questions, but instead it sounded like a question itself. It's scary, but I can almost literally see their minds working. The nameless girl has gone even paler and looks at me as if I am some kind of monster or something. Angela frowns at me disgustedly.

John's reaction is not even close to that of the others. His face is neither revolted nor terrified. His expression is blank, except for his green eyes. They stare at me searchingly as if trying to figure out whether I'm telling the truth or not. Though, granted, I would not believe myself either if I were him.

"So, what do we have to do next?" I ask, hoping at least John will catch the bait and change the subject, preferably in my favor. I try to send him a pleading mental message without having my face betray anything. John and I have never been buddy buddy or whatever, but from these three, he definitely seems like the most sensible and understanding. He looks at me for another agonizing moment.

"Guess we could start talking about our presentation. Any ideas?" He turns to the other two girls, and I let out the breath I wasn't aware of holding. Who knows, maybe a great friendship is on its way after all.

The rest of the day goes by in anxiety. Whenever someone says my name, I flinch. Whenever someone looks in my direction, I stare back as challengingly as I can manage, while hoping they can't hear how my heart is racing. Every whisper and every glance makes me uncomfortable. I'm paranoid of all the people around me; I see a shadow lurking in everyone's mind. The shadow of my past is the only thing I can focus on, the only thing I desperately wish to ignore.

As soon as the bell rang I stormed out of the classroom, afraid of being confronted not so much by Angela or the pale girl whose name I still can't remember, but by John. His insightful gaze had really scared me, and I really did not want to be cornered and questioned by him. Or anyone, for that matter.

I feel as if I'm being hunted. I'm the prey of my own past. My own dark past, which I know won't disappear but I at least hoped for it to be ignored. We'd been so careful to keep it all hidden. My parents had purposely chosen a treatment center in another state to make absolutely sure no one would know me. We'd prepared and rehearsed excuses in case I'd ever run into anyone at my therapist's office. My family had tried so hard to seal this part of my life and to lose the key which would open all the doors to my dark story. And despite pretending I didn't care if anyone would find out, I have to admit I was relieved that they took it so seriously and were so cautious. Switzerland was the perfect excuse for my absence. We had it all planned down to the very last detail. My mum had even written everything down on index cards. It was perfect, it was foolproof.

But of course I had to find a way to ruin it. Of course I just couldn't keep my big mouth shut. Of course it was all my fault. Again.

Sitting in Theresa's office, I think about telling her all of this. I think about voicing my fears, my concerns, my thoughts. I know that's what I'm supposed to do. It is part of the reason for these sessions. But despite knowing it all, I just sit there. I can neither meet her eyes, nor say a word. My throat feels constricted. In a way I want to cry but I know I won't. I never do in front of others. Tears are reserved for my darkest hours, alone in my room, alone in my universe.

She knows something is wrong, more than usually. She tries to pry, but just because it's her job. Theresa has learned a lot about me in these past months, including that if I don't want to talk, I won't. Only one question do I answer and only because I don't want her to cross the invisible line I draw at times like these. The line, as thick as steel and as fragile as my heart, that keeps everyone shut out when I need it, when I want it. At least that's the way I see it. To everyone else it's the cage I draw around myself. The distance I crave and defend if someone dares to cross it. I'm not just being paranoid about her not respecting it. She's done it before. Whenever Theresa has felt it necessary, she has come up, pushed back my sleeves, taken off my bracelets and inspected my wrists. But I don't want to be touched today, so I shake my head when she asks if I have done it again. I don't know why she believes me this time, but she does and that's all that matters in my bubble of silence.

The hour draggingly races by; it feels like an eternity, it feels like an instant. I don't know what it feels like and I don't care. Time doesn't matter, because I know it passes, no matter how stuck in the moment I may be. It always does.

"Time's up."

The weekend is long and short. Dark and bright. Here and there. Mine and not. I feel like I'm living in between two worlds, which I can't quite identify. Sometimes it's a mix of the past and the possible future. In those scenarios I can imagine all too vividly how my parents will react once they get a call from the headmistress informing them that they don't want a mentally ill person at their school. These phone calls mix in with the conversation my group and I had during English. But sometimes I'm ripped back to the present, to the fact that the phone is ringing, but no one seems concerned once they pick up. These are the moments that let me breathe, that take the edge off, but only for a moment. Only long enough until I remember that I'm not safe yet. That I really won't ever be safe again.

My nerves are electrified and I can barely sit still, until it all shifts into the other extreme. One minute I'm all jittery and the next I lie on my bed as still as a person would in a coffin and just reflect on my life.

It's hardest when my mother is around because she has the eagle eye. Or is just paranoid, my preferred terminology. On any given day she'll analyze each of my words, weighing them, trying to figure out their hidden meaning. It's quite amusing sometimes because I can't always predict when something will set her off. However, this weekend does not contain a single amusing or entertaining fiber. It's just grueling and exhausting. But no matter how tired I am, sleep is out of the question and so I spend the nights lying awake, waiting for sleep, despite knowing that it's like waiting for rain in the Sahara: pointless, as all there is is heat, sand and dryness, with not a single water drop in sight.

8

I splash cold water into my face, willing myself to look and be awake. I'm dead tired; it was simply too long a weekend. I hate it that fears and worries kept me up and restless. I replayed English literature class in my head so many times it felt like it was becoming the opening track to my life. I could smack myself for how stupid I was. I actually did smack myself. Not that it helped even the least. Not like it used to. The problem was still there. The conversation had happened nevertheless. Then again, maybe it isn't a problem. Maybe they think I'm a freak, that's it. Maybe.

I lift my head to look into the mirror above my sink. I study my face while carefully applying my makeup. I spend most of my time with my concealer. I try to hide the purple, bruises like shadows beneath my eyes. Cursing won't make them go away, but I can't help myself. Tiredness is always evident on my face. I tend to sleep so much less than I should anyway, so one night of restlessness leaves its marks. Sighing, I turn away from my own reflection. There is no point in obsessing over it. There never is. If only I had thought that way a few months ago. If only I hadn't cared about how I looked. If only I could have ignored shallow beauty. If only.

Walking downstairs I dread what's ahead. I may be a good actress, but not everyone is fool enough to believe the show I put on. Or maybe she is just too obsessed herself. Either way, convincing my mum of my well-being won't be easy. It never is, no matter how true or false.

I take a deep breath. While letting it out, a smile places itself on my lips. It's not the overly cheery kind I reserve for my friend. That would set mum off. This one is subtle and still a little tired. It makes me look excited and cheery for the day, without seeming exaggerated. It's well practiced and it's all I have right now.

"Good morning." I stroll into the kitchen, casually grabbing an apple off the counter.

"Good morning, honey. Just take whatever you want. I wasn't sure if you wanted bagels or cereals." She turns around at the sink to smile at me. I beam back at her, taking big bites off my apple while rummaging through the cupboards to prepare my breakfast. I feel her eyes on me as I pour the milk into my bowl of Lucky Charms. I don't react, just pretend I'm not noticing it and instead peacefully spoon the cereals into my mouth while absentmindedly "reading" the paper.

"Done?" I nod, pushing the now empty dish across the table. Now comes the part of the morning which will show me whether or not my smile was convincing enough. I hop off the chair and walk towards the doorway, where I turn to look at my mother.

"I'll go finish getting ready."

"We're leaving in 10, ok?" I nod, turning away from her. My senses are alert, waiting for the things that will give her away. I walk up the stairs and go into the bathroom to brush my teeth. Leaving the door open is not laziness, but a way for me to control her controlling me. I listen for any creaking steps, any shallow breaths … anything that would indicate her being on the same floor. But all that I hear is faint noises coming from the kitchen.

I breathe a sigh of relief and feel my body relax. While getting ready, I try to avoid looking into the mirror because I really do not want to see my face again. It has annoyed me once today already and that is enough.

I finish brushing my teeth and hair. It's quite difficult to style it without a mirror, so I just pull a brush through it a couple of times and let it fall loosely onto my shoulders. Then I go into my room, grab my bag and plaster the smile back on my face which will tell my mum that everything is alright, even though everything could be on the verge of falling apart.

I'm dreaming; I walk into a class and everybody stares at me. Each pair of eyes follows my every movement, scrutinizing me, observing me. I speak to people and they answer. I ask questions and they respond. What they say makes sense; it's normal. But when I look into their faces, something completely different is written there.

Their words are secrets everyone knows. Their smiles are codes for things everybody understands. They are all directed at me, but despite how involved I am, I'm still the outsider. I walk down hallways and hear voices but when I turn around no one is watching me. I try to catch people looking or talking in a certain way so I might be able to call them out on it, but it never happens. I swivel around whenever I think I hear my name, but it's hopeless. It's a typical dream; one where whatever you try to achieve is so close, but still so far out of reach. It's a dream I hate because it scares me. It terrifies me every single time. Dreams are supposed to tell you something, supposed to be something deep from within you. Some say they are a premonition, others claim they are your subconscious dealing with what happened during your day. I don't know how to read this dream, which is why it scared me. I don't want it to be a hunch of the future because it would mean that everything would be breaking apart. My chest constricts and all I want to do is wake up. I pinch myself, hard. And then I fall straight into the next nightmare; one that there is no waking up from. I fall straight into my worst fears, my darkest creatures of the night. I fall straight into reality.

Everyone wants to live their dream and I was no exception when I was younger. Guess this proves once again that you have to be careful what you wish for.

Walking into the cafeteria at lunch is the worst. I step through the doors alone because I had to put something into my locker. I feel my pulse, the steady beating of my heart. I hear the voices floating across the room. But underneath it all I hear something else. It's like an intake of a collective breath, everybody focusing on me. I swear I can see people freeze, staring at me before turning to their friends. I'm convinced I can hear my name in every conversation, accompanied by sly gazes in my direction. I try to spot my friends across the crowded room, try to catch someone's eye, but it's difficult to make out separate faces. They are all a blur of my deepest anxiety which had been merely a nightmare until now. I had been afraid of my secret coming out but did I actually believe it would? I'd managed to pretend and act and smile even when I was dying on the inside, so why couldn't I hide with the same skills once I was better?

Unsteadily I make my way to the salad bar. I pile things onto my plate, not even paying attention to what it is. I just focus on my breathing. I attempt to swallow, but my throat is raspy and dry. It feels as if my face will crack if I smile, but I know I have to. I know I have to go on even if it means facing my fears. Especially if it means facing my fears and the people who are my living nightmares. I force a smile onto my face. I try to relax my shoulders and take on a less tense walk while wandering through the cafeteria to find someone I know. I have to squint a few times before I can finally make out Hailey's bright green shirt, a few tables down from where I am standing. I walk towards them, while trying to keep it all upright. It's vital that I don't crack, that my façade doesn't crumble, that I stand strong. I walk towards my friends feeling as if I'm headed to my execution. And maybe I am, because if they've heard, then it's all gone. The life and secrets I owned, they'll all come tumbling down, burying me beneath. Just a few more steps until I know. Just a few more steps until I am there.

I watch my friends, the tight clustered group of them. There is a stillness hovering over their table despite their obvious conversation. Instead of the usual, small individual chatter, each of them has a sincere expression and they don't represent the chaotic, sweet group of people I'm used to. The teenagers at this table inhabit my friends' bodies, but each of them acts like a stranger.

Mike, who is sitting opposite Hailey, spots me first. His eyes rest on me for a split second before he leans forward just the slightest bit. His lips are moving fast, but I can't make out what he is saying despite being in earshot. I can't hear, but I can imagine. They are probably just hammering down the details of how best to bring it up, of how to make me confess.

His whisper abruptly turns into a loud mocking of Emily's neon yellow nail polish when I reach the table. As if on command, the scene becomes lively and vibrant. The tense, suspicious atmosphere from moments before seems to have vanished and they all act like their usual, crazy selves. It's as if someone had pressed a button or they were given new stage directions. Too bad I'm a pro when it comes to acting and too bad that I'm just not buying it.

"Kaya! Hey, we've missed you!" Not even Steve's voice betrays anything, but that doesn't mean I can bathe myself in safety. It's not like they would ask me point blank; they'd have to prepare me first.

"Sorry, had to make a detour to my locker", I offer lamely. They smile, but I see Hailey's insecure glance. I notice a certain mistrust in Steve's eyes, and from the corner of my eye I spot Claire and Mike exchange a glance. I see all of this happening, and yet I ignore it. They are not the only ones who can play this game.

I take a seat and wait until someone comes up with a topic. There is a moment of silence and I can feel the unspoken question that's lingering on everyone's tongue. Challengingly I lift my head to meet everyone's eyes. I stare them down, and each of them looks away as they almost reluctantly join in the dissing of some of our teachers. A few of my friends, Mike and Steve, flash me a fleeting smile before turning away. Others barely manage to return my stare. Emily meets my eyes for only a split sec-ond before turning to Josh next to her to dish on the absolutely unacceptable amount of homework her French teacher gave her. But even a split second can be enough because I see all I need to. I see the disgust, the question, the judgment. And it hurts me so much that the weight of it hits me right into my heart and I have to catch my breath before turning to Hailey.

She calmly looks back at me, her brown eyes fixed on mine. There is no disgust or judgment in them. I see traces of a question, but it's overshadowed by something much more powerful: concern and hurt. True, the question is there; the slight doubt that maybe all the gossip and rumors is exactly just that, gossip and rumors. But she knows me better, senses that there is something I haven't been telling her. Maybe my e-mails or phone calls were tipping her off all along unconsciously, or maybe she just knows me better than I want to admit.

She is worried about me, wants to know what is going on, but she also feels guilty. She is wondering why I didn't tell her, why I didn't feel like I could confide in her. And much more than that, she is working it out; I can almost see the wheels in her head spinning, putting together my absence and supposed trip to Switzerland with the things she's heard. Or maybe she has it all figured out already, I wouldn't put it past her. She may be very cheerful and crazy, but she is definitely not dumb. Still water runs deep after all.

To me it seems like a dramatic moment, but meanwhile, the rest of the world keeps spinning and even she looks down after just a few seconds. Not even my best friend has the guts to say out loud what is so clearly in her eyes and on her mind. Though maybe that is exactly the point: I don't need to hear it, I know it already. I know that she has her mind more or less set about what's been going on, but she wants me to deny it. She wants me to tell her that it's not true, that she is completely off. Hailey wants me to state that it's just another rumor like the many that spread through the school at any given moment. She may be my best friend but she doesn't want either of our worlds to come tumbling down. Too late for that, honey. It's happened; admitting is all that's left.

But I don't and instead participate in the conversation, pretending I don't have a clue about what is going on. Pretending I don't notice everyone looking at my wrists, trying to figure out how my skin looks underneath all of the bracelets which have accessorized my arms for as long as anyone of us can, or even want to remember.

9

I walk down the hallway, not seeing an end to it, as if I would have to walk to infinity until I finally reached where I didn't want to go. I've been dreading this the whole day. Entering the school was bad, break was worse, lunch was absolutely terrible, but this might just break me. It's been such a short time and it's already going to come crashing down. Good things don't last, I've definitely learned as much.

I'm glad that I didn't remember this biggest of all challenges much earlier because I would have been worried sick by the idea of everything being destroyed. I am worried sick by that idea. But I can't change it, only run away or face it. And I probably wouldn't get very far anyway because, let's face it, this is San Diego and without a car it's difficult to get anywhere. So all I'm left with is facing it.

Involuntarily I slow my step as I draw closer to the door. I don't know what is waiting for me, but I'm afraid to find out. He wasn't at lunch—he had band practice—but that sure as hell doesn't mean he was spared the gossip. Better get it over with before my heart rips apart in anticipation.

Taking a deep breath I more or less sprint the last few meters, slowing my pace while stepping into the classroom. All my senses are set on alert, ready to pick up even the slightest hint that would indicate what he is thinking or what emotions he might be hiding.

The first thing I notice is that he is not there. Our usual seats are empty. The gaping void seems to mock me, teasing me for my anxieties previous to this lesson. I scowl at the lab table, annoyed at him, myself and everyone.

The second thing I notice is that everybody is staring. I feel their eyes on me, burning holes through my jewelry, while trying to get a glimpse of the delicate skin of my wrists. Fat chance.

"Oh jeez", I murmur to myself. The hurt and suffocating feelings of this morning have given way to annoyance. That's all I feel and I'm thankful for it. Annoyance is, well, not a good feeling, but better and more bearable than any of the others. It gives me an attitude of "I couldn't care less", which, under the current circumstances, is a complete lie, but far better than the truth. Because if I had to confess to what I really feel deep in my heart then I would probably break down sooner rather than later.

I purse my lips disapprovingly as I plop down on my chair. Letting my hair cover part of my face, I take out my school planner and commence scribbling to avoid the curious or disgusted or fascinated or whatever looks of my oh-so subtle classmates.

An angry line here, an exasperated scribble there. I decorate the page with hearts and words, absentmindedly tracing patterns that I had drawn there earlier.

Where is he? Despite my best efforts, I can't suppress the worry that's rising inside of me. The first bell has already gone and he is never late. What if something happened? What if, while I was freaking out about some silly, ridiculous rumor, he was being brought to the hospital in an ambulance? Ok, calm down, he is probably just simply late. Happens to the best of us.

I sit on the edge of my chair, nervously shooting glances at the door. I'm willing it to open, willing him to step inside. I try magical thinking, visualizing him coming in in as much detail as I can. The stressed look in his eyes, but nonetheless, the smile that he always sports. I picture his swift, confident walk while imagin-ing him making his way to our desk. I'll act cool, of course, and pretend that absolutely nothing is wrong. I'll act as if I hadn't even noticed his absence.

Suddenly the door swings open. I quickly focus on my scribbles again, trying to appear as if I couldn't care less, even though every nerve of my body is waiting for his closeness. Trying to act just like I'm supposed to.

"Sorry I'm late, but I had a meeting. Took longer than I thought." My body goes cold at the sound of the voice, which definitely does not belong to Tim. Slowly I look up, not even bothering to hide the hostility that must be showing in my face.

"Something wrong, Kaya?"Yup, as clear as cut glass.

"Bad day", I mumble, ignoring the message-heavy glances that my classmates exchange. I could kick myself for that stupid comment but I'm too absorbed by worrying about him. Now I'm definitely allowed to be concerned. Hence I don't hear the teacher's response, nor do I really care. What does it matter if I'm told off or if I didn't catch that I was told to open my book on a certain page if he is probably in the emergency room, hooked to some IVs while the doctors are contemplating how to save his precious life? Oh gosh, what if he won't survive? No, he's young and dynamic; I'm sure he'll be able to fight it. What a silly, petty girl I am. I imagine an ordinary scenario and actually spend moments of my life thinking about how best to act cool, when he might be struggling just to stay conscious.

I'm so preoccupied by my dark thoughts that I don't even hear the door open or see someone slip in quietly. Vigorously biting my lip, I jump a little when I feel a warm hand on my arm. Thousands of tiny, electric shocks rush through my veins, setting my skin on fire. His touch burns right through my shirt. The fire is so sudden and intense I don't want it to stop. It's exactly what I've been looking for all along. It's strong and stings right through my body until it pierces my heart. Yet still it's not enough. I turn my head to look at him. I want to assess if he looks hurt or in pain, or whether I can see any other explanation for his absence, but all

I can do is stare. I stare right into his beautiful eyes. The blue is clear, only rarely broken by grey specks, but even their color seems faded and dominated by the blue. I see him smile at me and my insides warm, the heat still pulsing through my veins. And then, all of a sudden, it grows cold. The longest second of my life turns into a mere memory. My blood turns colder, any form of pain is sucked out of me as my skin cools without his scorching touch. All that stays is his whispered "Hey" that lingers between us like the warmth on your skin when you walk out of the sun.

"Where were you?" My voice sounds sharper than intended. I regret it immediately and try to undo it by smiling sweetly.

"I was worried, you know."

"Ya, I'm sure you were. I mean, I was late a total of," he glances at his watch before looking back at me, "three whole minutes. You must have really gone through hell." His tone is mocking, but if only he knew …

"Idiot", I mumble, slapping his knee. He pretends to be writhing in pain which looks plainly ridiculous seeing as he is a terrible actor. Nevertheless, a giggle escapes my lips. I'm surprised at myself, how easy it somehow is to—for just a moment—forget everything that happened that day, to just joke around and have fun … But it is just a moment and it doesn't last. My smile wavers and then vanishes for just a split second before returning more brightly and by far less real than before.

Our teacher's stern look makes Tim sit up straight and put on a serious face, but the dimple in his cheek betrays him. I can see his eyes twinkling and it's difficult to make myself look away, but I know I have to.

"You never did answer my question …" I grumble. I don't have to watch his face to know that he is smiling, that the cute dimple in his cheek is visible and that his eyes are glowing with amusement. I just know it and that is worse than actually seeing it.

"I'm sorry, Your Royal Highness. I didn't mean to ignore your question. Band practice took longer than expected. And that's also where I was, Your Majesty." His tone is serious, but I can detect the slightest note of mockery within it. And, though it's childish, I can't help but stick my tongue out at him.

"Hm, I mistook you for the princess. Seems like you're just an ordinary fool of the court, my mistake." I gape at him for a moment, unable to come up with a witty response. He just called me a princess! A princess, her majesty and your royal highness! He thinks I'm royal!

Then the diss of his comment sinks in, and I squint at him playfully menacingly. I try to bare my teeth at him, but—judging from his grin—it doesn't seem to have quite the right effect.

"Don't make me hurt you again. You know I would." He pretends to be terrified, but again fails horribly. We both break out into laughter, no longer able to hold it back. And just like that, my smile is real and I'm happy. Well, happy is a big word, but at least not devastated. Just normal.

"If you two are done not paying attention, then please open your books at page 154 and answer the questions up until number 5." The teacher looks at us sternly and only now do I notice everyone's eyes watching us. Of course, people's stares have been following me all day long, but this time they are not only disgusted and shamelessly curious—though there are some of those as well—but also simply annoyed at our interruption.

We both silently open our books. I see him get engrossed in the page, absentmindedly biting on his pen. I try to concentrate on the task ahead, but my focus keeps shifting to Tim. From the corner of my eye, I watch him occasionally highlight a phrase. When he's done, he writes the title on a blank piece of paper and starts answering the questions. His writing is a bit scribbly, like most guys I know, but it's still legible.

With his head bowed over the book, I can study his profile well. The sudden urge to touch him overcomes me and is all-consuming. It feels impossible to resist. He is so close and every nerve in my entire body is sensitively aware of it. I could just reach out and stroke his face, touch his arm or clasp his warm, strong hand in mine. I could just overcome the distance between us with one small movement. I imagine how his skin must feel, whether his hands are soft or a little rough. Would he pull away? Or would he hold my hand in his and let me feel the pain that would inevitably radiate through my whole body like thousand fires racing through my veins straight into my heart?

For the rest of the lesson, I try hard to keep my eyes averted from his beautiful face and his gorgeous body. My whole body is fighting the urge to touch or at least look up at him. I go against all I want, and it feels like the longest fight of my life until the bell finally rings, dismissing us. Only now do I allow myself to smile up at him and bathe in his warm gaze for a few delicious seconds before leaving the classroom to head to my next hour of torture.

My cell vibrates on the bedside table. I pick it up, checking who's trying to reach me. I don't really have the energy for anyone.

"Whatsapp Message from Tim W." Tim W. Biology Tim? Why would he have my number? Or, why would he text me in the first place? I click on it, intrigued.

> **Hey, Kaya. It's Tim. Do you know what bio hmrwk is?**
> **Hey! Yup, I do ;) How'd you get my nr?**
> **Haha, from Mike. Willing to share your knowledge with me?**
> **Haha hm … lemme think about that …**
> **Please?**

Well, if you're begging…lemme go check

Ok

It's p. 128 Nr. 1,3,4 and 7.

Ok, thank you!

No worries, anytime.

I might actually take you up on that.

Anytime ;)

See you tomorrow. Bye!

Bye-bye! xx

10

My room is dark, all the lights are out and the closed curtains block out any source of light that could find its way into the darkness from the outside. The darkness isn't a monster that could capture and eat me, nor is it a black prison surrounding me. There's no movement within that could be detected because it doesn't live. It doesn't breathe. All it does is take my breath away, make me suffocate. If someone came into my room right now then all they'd have to do is to hit the light switch. Electricity would provide them with light in this dark room. But even with a spotlight on me or the entire sun crammed into my bedroom, darkness still wouldn't shift for me. It would still be here, lurking beneath my skin, within my heart and soul. It would dim the light, because no source of illumination is ever powerful enough to fight it. It's all-consuming. It cra-dles me like a child, but there is no comfort. There is just a never ending battle.

I'm the child of a deaf mother who doesn't hear me scream. I can yell and cry and scream as long and loud as I want to, no one will hear because darkness muffles the sounds. It takes them away, makes them irrelevant. It mutes everything until merely the exhaustion of my inner pain is left. And even then it doesn't leave but just waits for my next rush of energy, for my next attempt at a battle that's already lost.

I stare into the darkness of the room. I know where my bed stands, my desk and which clothes are strewn about on the floor. I know it but I can't see it.

I listen. My breathing is uneven, forced and shallow. My heart is beating wildly, while at the same time barely having a pulse. The beats are heavy and strong, threatening to pound right out of my chest. Nevertheless, I can't hear it. I feel it, like the underlining beat of the moment, but it doesn't make a sound. Or maybe it does and I just can't detect it. Maybe in reality my breaths are the beat and my heart is the sound. Or maybe it's all muted and I'm just imagining everything.

The silence in the room is so overwhelmingly loud that I press my hands to my ears to make it stop. I don't want to hear it. I don't want to see it and I don't want to feel it. Because all I want is to hear, to see and to feel. I want, but I don't. I'm lost and yet no one is looking for me.

A wave of despair washes over me so unexpectedly that I gasp inaudibly. It hits me so strongly, I double over. I just slide down the wall onto my knees. My fingers find their way into my hair and grip it tightly. I press my face into my sweater and just want it to end. Another wave rolls over me and I bite the fabric until my teeth hurt and the taste of my Abercrombie sweater fills my mouth. The fabric gets soaked by my silent tears and for a brief moment I wonder if I could drown in it. But just as soon as I think it, another bomb of pain explodes inside of me making me cringe again. I feel the pain and despair building up inside of me, to the point of almost making me burst. I want to get rid of it, release it, but I can't. I won't. I should.

Exhausted, I roll onto my back. My vision is clouded by a curtain of wet, pained tears. According to someone, tears are words that the heart can't express. I know how that feels.

The pain in my chest is numbed, overcome by simple exhaustion. My limbs are heavy and I'm so tired it feels like I could sleep forever, without ever waking up again.

I can't move, nor do I want to. I just lie there, letting my heart tell the story that no one can hear until I drift into a restless sleep, seemingly without a beginning, but a definite ending.

11

I'm tired. I'm exhausted. My eyes are a bit swollen from crying and my skin is pale despite the foundation and rouge I used to try to cover it. There are purple blueish shadows under my eyes and I swear I look like I might be auditioning for the part of a vampire in the "Twilight Saga". Maybe not even such a bad idea, with all my brilliant acting I might even land it. And then I'd move to Hollywood, become one of those over-night starlets whose secrets are even juicier than the diet shakes they drink to stay in shape. At least until the press discovers what I'm hiding and reveals it to the whole damn world. On second thoughts, maybe not such a great plan after all.

I sigh, letting my make-up kit slip back into my Christian Audigier bag. It was a Christmas gift and I remember smiling and hugging my aunt when she got it for me though, inside, I didn't feel more than a second of excitement. I mean I love the bag. It's edgy and cool. Black leather covered in golden studs with the typical logo on the front and a silver lining all around. Nevertheless, it's just a bag, which is never enough to make it all go away. Never enough to save me from myself.

I push the dark thoughts out of my mind, determined to make the best of this day. One step—one day—

at a time. It's what Theresa keeps telling me. It doesn't matter what was yesterday and I should not care what will be tomorrow. The moment is what counts; the moment is all I can handle. And yet, sometimes even that seems too much. Sometimes even a moment seems like eternity. Whenever that happens, I try to tell my self that another moment is just another moment away. Too bad that that also brings another eternity, another forever of fights and battles with myself.

The bathroom door swings open and I watch in the mirror as Ruby walks in, head held high and shoulders rolled back. She stands next to me and looks at herself, admiring her reflection while she flips her dirty blond hair once this, once that way. She pouts at herself in the mirror and bats her eyelashes. I've seen her do this a thousand times, be it as practice or for real. In her mind, the world revolves around her. She is the most amazing, incredible, fabulous person and she wants everyone to know it. In her mind, I'm just another tool, disguised as a friend.

"Oh my gosh, Kaya. I didn't even see you there." Leaning in, she swiftly hugs me. A whiff of her perfume fills my nose and it's hard to return her smile. It's hard because, looking at her, it's obvious that we both know how fake the other's easy going cheerfulness is. We both know that we're not really friends and yet we both keep up the façade.

"No offense, but you look kind of tired … is everything ok?" Her face is concerned and if I didn't know her better, I may even believe it. But I do know her and hence it's easy to spot the glimmer in her eyes. The one she tries to hide but just can't. Fake people have that trait. No matter how good they may be at acting, their real intentions can rarely be completely hidden. A twitching of the lips, a gleam in the eyes, an inappropriate smile … there is always a giveaway, you just need to learn to spot it. I learned it fast and the hard way. I learned because time after time I trusted her, relied on her and time after time she let me down, took me down. But still, here we are, pretending to be friends. Granted, she is too ignorant to realize that I see right through her, but really what does it matter?

I can't remember thinking of her even once during my absence, and yet it's just like before. Now that I think about it, she must be devastated that I'm back. The moment she heard that I had returned—or at the very latest the moment she saw me in the cafeteria—was the exact moment she started coming up with a plan to make my life harder, to put me in my place. Ruby is just so transparent once you know the real her.

And because I do, I know what she is after. I know that she has heard the rumours, I know that she suspects them to be true. She is probably the one spreading most of it. This is the opportunity she has been hoping for. The thing with which she can take me down, prove her point and put me in my place. And yet I stand here like a complete idiot, smiling, claiming everything is fine and I just stayed up too late. Listening to her too sweet voice telling me that she is always here if I need someone to talk to. Telling me lie after lie.

When the bell rings and she stalks out to rush to class, I lean against the cool wall. I feel hollow, burnt and empty. A wave of exhaustion washes over me and it takes a lot of magical thinking to make me stand up straight and then walk down the now empty hallway to my next class, to my next hour of wishing I was somewhere else.

"I hate my life right now. There, I said it. Confidentiality though, so not a word." Theresa looks at me. Just looks at me, her face as blank as an unpainted canvas. Her expression is smooth, flawless of any disturbing emotions that could ruin the perfect façade of blankness. I had expected, hoped even, to see some kind of feelings on her face. To see even just a twitch of her mouth, a sparkle in her eyes. Even disgust may have been better than nothing, better than the way I see her face now.

The silence between us stretches out. Suddenly I'm not so sure telling her was a good idea. I know she is my therapist and all, but really I'm just here because it makes my parents feel in control. It makes them believe I'm safe and sound and better. She's not being paid for actually being a friend and helping me, she's being paid for

making my parents sleep better at night and for keeping her mouth shut.

"No comment? I thought you are supposed to be my
therapist who helps me talk about things and stuff." Her
eyes don't leave mine and I try to challenge the words
out of her. Why won't she say anything? Why does she
leave me hanging?

"Hellooooooo? Anybody home?" I wave my hand in
front of me, not bothered enough yet to get up and actually wave it in front of her face directly. Theresa simply
raises an eyebrow.

"That's all? No further reaction? Seriously? What kind of
a crappy therapist are you?" My voice is high pitched and
I feel my cheeks flushing. A hot flame of anger flares up in
the pit of my stomach. I close my eyes for a second, trying
to suppress the boiling bubbles inside of me. I try a few
deep breaths, but they can't calm me. I squeeze my eyes for
another moment, hoping I will be able to save myself—
and Theresa—from the worst. Too bad it's too late.

So fast I can barely even see it coming, I jump off the
couch and glare at Theresa.

"What the hell? Are you trying to make me mad?
Cause it sure as hell is working!" Still, she just looks
at me. Not even my outburst brought up any reaction
within her. I swear that woman is made of stone! Cold,
unmovable stone.

"I cannot believe you!" In a fresh burst of anger I grab
the tissue box off the table and hurl it at her. And though

I miss pathetically, I would really have expected her to do something at that. Even if it is yelling at me. My hands are slightly shaking and I'm panting. My cheeks are hot and tears suddenly spring into my eyes. A painful jab of feeling unloved and uncared for hits my stomach and makes me want to curl up on the couch and give in to the sobs that threaten to erupt from my chest.

"Don't you care? Are you another one of those people who couldn't care less whether or not I'm alive?" My voice breaks on the last word and I bite my lip in anger. A metallic taste fills my mouth but it's unwanted and not even the sharp pain in my lip is satisfying.

Theresa looks at me. What a mess of a girl I must portray. I don't even want to imagine what my makeup must look like, yet alone delve into the fact that I lost my cool, that I gave up my poker face.

"Are you done?" Her words fill the static air and float to reach me through my bubble of crazy anger.

"Oh sure, now you can suddenly speak." I can't hide the bitterness in my voice; I'm too exhausted to even try. Not caring about looking weak, I let myself fall back onto the couch with a defiant sigh.

"Kaya, I'm sorry." She pauses and looks at me. "And though it must not have been pleasant at least you gave in to your emotions. It's a big step; you didn't suppress them. How did that feel?"

Of course; I should have known it was another one of her sneaky little exercises. Isn't it always?

"I don't know. I felt … abandoned by you. I thought you were supposed to help me, not make me feel worse." Sliding the bracelets up and down my wrist, I add as almost an afterthought: "Sorry for chucking the tissues at you, by the way." Theresa smiles at me and suddenly it all seems better. Her face is back to normal, back to something moveable and changeable. I'm glad the emotionless mask is gone because it scared me.

"I pretty much provoked it, so no worries. So when you felt abandoned, did that remind you of something?" I am about to raise an eyebrow at her when I suddenly— well, not exactly have a flashback, but it's more than a memory as well. I recognize the feeling inside; the jab of being unloved and uncared for. Trying to place it, I search my brain for something to associate with it. There are lots of times I've felt that way, many times I've felt abandoned by the people I care for. But none of those moments seems to fit.

"Mhm … I guess." She waits for me to say more, waits for me to have that moment of revelation. I try hard to please her, try hard to remember. I rack my brain. It's kind of funny how much people and views on something can change. When I first started coming here I spent most of my time singing songs in my head, trying to look like I was concentrating when I was really only trying to kill some time. Now I have realized that she actually can help me and that I do feel better sometimes, or that the darkness is at least not too suffocating permanently.

I think about those months before that day that changed it all. I felt unloved a lot. Useless, not worthy of anyone. I did feel like most people were turning on me and like there was no point in anything. But abandonment was never really part of it because I wanted to be alone. I was the one who pulled back and who locked herself away from others and the hatred that I felt was directed purely at me.

I tiptoe around the actual day it happened and focus instead on the months afterwards. And suddenly it hits me.

"It felt like after. Like, when I had to see doctors and therapists and all that stuff." I remember exactly how my parents made me visit many different specialists, but no one ever seemed to say anything different. I remember their faces always being hopeful and fearful at the same time. They hoped I would be cured and they were terrified for me.

"My parents", I whisper. Now that it's out, it hangs in the air. I feel the truth of the statement, the weight of it that threatens to bury me beneath. I silently shake my head, trying to forget about this thought, trying to ignore what's so clearly in front of me right now. I used to be so good at ignoring and suppressing things, but Theresa has broken me. With every honest session it got harder. Every time I opened up, I lost a bit of this ability.

Feeling the wetness run down my cheeks, I suddenly notice the silent tears I'm weeping. She offers me the tissues and I take them thankfully though I'm too absorbed to even show my gratitude.

My parents suffocate me by protecting me. I never wanted to hurt them, only me. I never wanted to inflict pain on them, they were never my target. And yet it feels like they're punishing me for everything I did to them by doing something to myself. They abandoned me because the girl they thought I was died the day I didn't. They are too scared to face me. Too scared to confront it themselves.

"They'll never see, will they?" My question is shaky and it takes a lot of courage to lift my head and look into Theresa's eyes. She looks back at me, her eyes resting on mine.

"Do you really want them to?"

12

I'm absorbed by something far beyond the backyard. I can see the little pond in the corner, the wooden fence surrounding the whole property, the patio with the table made of black steel. Yet, my eyes and mind are far away, focused on places I can't see from here. I've been there, seen it. My hands wander across the picture album on my lap. The pages are colorful and filled with memories we once thought were important to hold onto. My parents probably still see it that way, but I have learned that all that really matters is what you felt every step along the way because that is all you'll get to keep. In those moments before I picked up the knife, I hadn't bothered to take out all my picture albums and old schoolwork and flick through them. I had just let the most beautiful, most memorable moments run through my mind. I wanted to hold onto them even on the other side. Photographs are fun to take but, in the long run, they mean nothing.

I look at a picture of me on a beach in front of a speed boat. I'm in full diving gear and I'm smiling. My blond hair is tousled by the wind and the salt water didn't do it any good either, but I look happy. You can't see Hailey on the picture, but she was there too. It was taken in Ile Maurice and we had both just gotten back from our first dive ever. I love scuba diving. I have since the very first session in the pool. I love being underwater, feeling the cold current in my hair. Everything is so calm and peaceful down there. I feel completely at ease, as if I have always belonged there. You're not an intruder into that world like when you go snorkeling, but instead you're actually a part of it. The fascinating fish and the landscape are just magnificent, not necessarily that colorful, but it all seems so right. I can taste the salt on my lips, feel the pure water on my skin. Sitting on the ocean bottom is an incredible feeling. Being there, 30 meters under water, sitting cross-legged on sand and looking up at the surface. I can see the light and I know how it looks up there, but I'm removed from it, part of a different world. There are barely any sounds and it's the closest I've ever gotten to meditation because I never really follow through on any thought process. It's the only time I can fully shut down my mind and just be. The tranquility and beauty of it all, that's how I imagine death to be. Nothing will seem to matter anymore, you just are. Maybe not in a physical sense, but in your purest essence. A beam of light, a weightless soul.

Turning the pages, memories flood my mind. Hailey and me making silly model poses at the beach at night; my parents and me all dressed up at a restaurant; Hailey and me in the water surrounded by dolphins. Page by page, memory by memory. I'm smiling on most of them. Even when I'm not, I still seem oddly happy. It surprises me every time. I don't know how I could pull it off, how I found it in me to lie to everyone who looks at these photographs. Have I become that dishonest?

I turn over another heavy page. The picture on that one is of Hailey and me again. It's amazing how often she is featured in my album, but that's Hailey. She was that girl's closest friend. That girl who always smiles into the camera and only bled behind locked doors.

I smile at the picture. I remember that moment, that night, exactly. We are posing on our balcony. Our hair had been done by professionals that day; hers is studded with pearl-like clips while mine is swept to the side in a curly ponytail held in place by Swarovski encrusted hairpieces. We were so excited, looking forward to our very first ball. It was a charity event and we sold lottery tickets, but we felt like princess when we were getting ready in my bathroom together.

We've had so many of those days, times we got ready together, our make-up spread out everywhere. We'd do each other's face sometimes, or simply watch the other, hoping we would learn something we didn't already know.

Thinking of Hailey makes my throat feel tight. In the short time I've been back, there have been moments when I already feel miles away from her. She held me when I cried, was by my side when I had an embarrassing moment and laughed along with me. Her laughter and mine, one and the same on so many occasions. We used to be in our own bubble, just her and me against the rest. That's the way it used to be. And now it's me against the world, me in a bubble of my own, her on the outside, trying to look in.

It's been months since that one day that changed everything in my world. Then again, was it really just that day's fault? Is it fair of me to blame it completely? It wasn't that the day had taunted me, making me hurt myself, making me wish to disappear. I had been playing with the thought for a while, pushing it around my mind. The desire had been boiling up inside of me more frequently. Yes, I was terrified of pain. Was back then, still am. I hate injections and taking blood and nearly fainted before piercing my ears. But that was different. I knew I was going to kill myself—how else would I escape my life?—but it was a different feeling. Theoretically and logically speaking I knew that the way towards my freedom, my happiness, was by taking my own life. That was a fact, a means to an end. The real purpose though wasn't that at all. I just merely wanted to be free, to breathe and not be restrained by my own life. I didn't want to kill myself; I wanted what came after. But instead, I was found and people saved me even though I would have begged them not to. That's the thing: I know that some people secretly do want to be saved and helped and cared for; it's like their cry for help. Not for me. For me it was my exit because no

one had heard my cries for help. They were silent—
I never screamed because hurting myself was never
something negative. It was relief, it was dangerous, it was
the point where I secretly did want to be saved.

People tell me that I should learn to talk about it, to
tell my friends and family how I feel. I should treat it as
something I learned from. Basically, they want me to lie.
Despite their attempt at disguising it as "honesty." But I
can't. Because though I do feel better, I also feel worse.
It took me quite a while to realize it, but I think the
medication is to blame. They stabilize my mood while
plunging me into further despair. It is supposed to hit
me less but, when it does, then hard core. I should tell
people about it; Theresa, my parents, the doctor. I keep
vowing I will but I never do. Yes, being miserable sucks,
big time. But it's also something I know, something I'm
familiar with. In a strange, masochistic way I like feeling
down. Every time it happens it kills me inside out, but
at least it's something to hold onto. That feeling—the
hollowness, the pain—it's what has imprinted my life so
strongly over the past few years and only when it's there
do I feel truly like myself. Even thinking it, it sounds
sick. But as they say: truth is stranger than fiction, no
matter how much we like to pretend otherwise.

I shut the album and just sit there, staring at my wrist.
I can't see the flesh but I know it better than my face.
Bracelets hide the scars but only from the eyes of others.

I know better. The pale lines forever embedded in my skin are all of my doing. They are the best, as well as the worst of those dark months. The pain and the relief in one. The end and the beginning combined.

So many times have I let my finger follow the lines, tracing patterns of pain and relief. I could trace them on anybody's wrists by now. I want to trace them on someone else's wrist; see if they fit anybody's skin or just mine. I often wonder if the beauty of those faint white lines is visible to my eyes alone. I don't like when people romanticize self-harm. It's not romantic, it's sad. But somehow those white lines are beautiful anyway. Or maybe I'm just crazy.

13

I can do this. It's going to be alright. Yes, everything is going to be ok. I wish, I dream, I know it won't work. No matter how much I try to convince myself that it's going to go great, I can't imagine it. She loves me, sure, but can love conquer even this? She is big on trust and keeping this from her for such a long time—I don't know how well she'll take it. But maybe that's exactly the point. Maybe I'm trying to prove to my parents that communication doesn't make everything better, no matter how much people try to insist. Words can be beautiful and powerful, but they can't turn back time and fix things.

Looking at myself in the mirror once more, I take a deep breath. Inhaling and exhaling slowly, while imagining all negativity leaving my body. I can do this.

I leave the bathroom, careful not to touch the doorknob. Stepping outside, the Californian sun hits me immediately and I thankfully get to hide my eyes behind my shades. I slender down the outdoor hallways, peeking into shop windows along the way. It's been a long while since I've been here and I've missed it. I love malls, especially outdoor ones. I used to spend lots of time in places like this with my friends and my mum; window shopping, actually shopping, hitting Starbucks, checking out cute guys. It's part of how I grew up, part of my home.

I breathe in the air that is so special to me. It's hard to describe. Warm and fresh and salty and good and dry and just perfect. The sun shines onto my bare arms and I love hearing the flopping sound people's shoes make. There are mothers and daughters, dressed almost alike. Some have business-like faces as if shopping is the biggest task and burden in their day, while others just look relaxed as they slender along. I side step a cluster of giggling girls, each holding a bag from Abercrombie. They remind me so much of my friends and me in their short shorts and colorful t-shirts.

Even though I purposely used the restroom at the other end of the mall, I arrive at the food court much too quickly. Every step taking me closer was one I dreaded. I look around, hoping I'll spot her while fearing it at the same time.

"Looking for someone?" Her voice next to my ear makes me jump. I hurl around, glaring at her. Her dirty blond hair is tied into a bun and she is wearing a tank top, jeans cut offs and flip flops. Without looking, I know that the glittering "H" is dangling around her neck on its silver chain. I've known this girl for ages. This is Hailey, my best friend. She'll understand.

"Funny to run into you here." I smile and return her hug—carefully.

"I know! What a 'coincidinc'!" Her giggle sounds a bit like a six-year-old's and it's just so contagious, I can't help but giggle along.

"So what does madam feel like?" She links her arm through mine and before I even get the words out, she is already pulling me towards the smoothie bar. I laugh, feeling light hearted. Strange how fast everything can change. When before it all seemed like some murky shade, it's now pure and brighter. Memories of the way life used to feel flood my memory and invade my heart.

"Am I that predictable?"

"Hon, after 12 years—ya, you are!" She smiles at me as we push through the door. A waft of cool air welcomes us and I breathe in the refreshing smell of fruits. It's loud and my mum hates the noise of the mixer along with the chattering of all the customers, but to me it is great. It's familiar, it's something I love. We stand in line, discussing which smoothie option sounds the most appealing. I watch Hailey laugh, retie her bun, throw her arm around me. Even though I still tense when she touches me, I feel myself relax at the same time. I love feeling so normal; it's something I was craving without knowing it. I feel something close to happiness rising in my heart, filling my soul and body with calmness.

We order our smoothies—raspberry, banana, strawberry for her and peach, coconut, raspberry and banana for me—and laugh together when they call out our order for "Harry and Hermione". She is still giggling about the expression of some on the other customers' faces as we find an empty table outside and take a seat.

I lean back in the sun, warming my bare arms and face. The voices of the other people around us fade into a soothing background hum, and her voice is the only one that matters. I answer back, talk to her, engaged in our conversation about … who knows? Because that is the beauty of best friends. You don't know what you talk about and if someone asked me, even if my life depended on it, I don't know if I could recall our topics. Random things, thoughts popping into our heads. Sometimes they are linked to each other, sometimes they are seemingly plucked out of air. It's like this huge spinning wheel that can land on any field at any moment.

I savor the taste of my smoothie; try to pick out certain tastes. I love how all the flavors are mixed when you first take a sip, but then one after another gradually melts away until only one is left. Sometimes it's peach or raspberry or coconut. But each time it's delicious and refreshing and normal.

Suddenly my phone vibrates on the table. I try to reach for it, but Hailey is faster. She snatches it away from me.

"Tim?" My best friend squints at me, raising her eyebrows.

"May I please have my phone?"

"Hm … in a sec." I sigh, knowing there is not much I can do about it. She types in my password. Her eyes scan whatever he wrote me and she passes me the phone with a frown.

"So not exciting."

"Sorry to disappoint."

Hey! What's up?

"Kaya! Quality time … no phones!"

"Sorry, sorry. I'm gonna get rid of him real quick, ok?"

"Emphasis on 'quick'."

Girl time with Hailey – No boys allowed ;)

Oh, I can take a hint! So this is how rejection feels.

Well, the younger you learn it, the easier life gets.

I'm taking your word for it!

Haha, maybe you shouldn't

Too late

G2g ttyl?

Idk, if I've gotten over the pain of your rejection by then …

I heard there are groups for that

Burn! ;) ttyl xx

Ttyl xx

"No more phones, promise."

After a while—or maybe a few hours, I don't really care—we get up. Strolling over to the trash can to toss away our empty cups, she links her arm through mine

and we walk that way all through the mall and into
M.A.C. where Hailey wants to buy a lipstick.

We're probably driving the lady behind the counter crazy as we try on various different shades of pink and red, rejecting some and further considering others. We ask her about the textures and effects of each and then—after a minute of silence so that she can overthink her choice again—she buys a young shade of pale pink.

"What a success, my dear." I laugh at Hailey's failed imitation of a British accent and counter in my own best version of it:

"Absolutely so. As much as I enjoyed it, I need to be heading home. Is your mom picking you up?" Her grin spreads and I burst out laughing at her Texan accent.

"Sure thing, gal. I just gotta give her a ring and she'll be here." We're both still smiling as we take out our cell phones, dial their numbers and ask for a ride.

"Pick up in 20?"

"Yup."

"Thinking what I'm thinking?" She smiles cheekily as we say at the same time: "Starbucks!"

It suddenly hits me how much I missed this. Thinking alike, shouting things at the same time, laughing at random things and seemingly not having a care in the world. I know that it is not true and that I will have to face it all eventually, but seeing her shake her head laughingly, I can't bring myself. I can't make myself tell her the truth, the reason why I wanted to meet. All along, my intention of confessing everything to her was actually very selfish. Who am I to ruin her probably quite good day? Who am I to make her worry about me and swear her to secrecy about something as dark as my story? I have already hurt and disrupted the life of my parents and my family, no need to do the same to my friends. Especially not my best friend, the girl who was always there for me. It's not her fault she isn't in the picture about everything that has happened or what I have been through. She didn't run away from me, I was the one pushing her away. Yet still she didn't abandon me.

I don't deserve a friend like her. She tries to be a good friend and a good person, and she is indeed one of the sweetest people I know. That's her. And I was willing to hurt her and throw it all away the moment I opened the drawer and took out that knife.

I'm so ungrateful. I don't deserve people caring for me so much. I don't even regret it.

"Baby, what's wrong?" I look at Hailey, her features blurry. I didn't even realize that I had started crying, but now I can't stop. Tears are flooding my eyes and running over my cheeks. I can't control myself as sobs ripple through me, shaking my whole body. I want to tell her that it's all good, that I'm just having such a good time. Anything. But I can't, I just keep crying. Shame tints my cheeks scarlet and I turn away, my hair falling over my face. I hate having people see me cry. It betrays my weakness. My dark secrets, a hint of everything that I'm trying to hide inside.

"It's going to be ok, I promise. It's fine, everything is ok. You're back with me, babes!" I hear Hailey's smile through her whispered words. Her scent surrounds me, invades my every pore. It's the Hailey scent I've known for years. Not her perfume, but something underneath it. Something more her, more personal. It's like home; it envelops me beautifully, like holding your favourite teddy from many years ago. Gosh, I missed this girl.

I can't tell how much time goes by while we just stand there hugging each other somewhere in Fashion Valley between MAC and Starbucks. This is why I love her so much: she doesn't need words to understand me. Which, of course, is the exact reason why I distanced myself from her so strongly. Even though she was never able to put her finger on it, I could tell she sensed that something was going on with me. And it made me feel guilty. Her "Kaya, what's wrong?" pierced straight to my heart and hurt me so much. Looking into her eyes became a challenge and the days before I tried to end it all, it was rare. Could she read what I was thinking? Could she tell how I felt? It was agony. She was a reason I almost didn't do it. I was so worried and afraid of how it would affect her. I was scared she'd blame herself for my death. That she would keep thinking, if only she had seen the signs and interpreted them correctly. If only she had stayed with me more often, occupied me. If only … Yet I did it, because I am so selfish and my own release was more important than she was.

I remember the last time I saw her. Well, the day I wanted to die. We were in the hallway after school. It was loud and crowded. I wanted to get out of there. I felt suffocated. I couldn't look anyone in the eyes. I was hiding from it all. I hadn't set my mind in the sense of "I'm going to kill myself today", but I felt that I was at a breaking point; I couldn't go on and keep pretending. I didn't actively know what I was going to do once I got home but I somehow felt that something inside of me had shifted. I remember walking towards the double doors that lead out of the school building. My bag was slung over my shoulder; the vibrant pink standing in such contrast to the black that covered my heart. My stare was fixed on those doors. I didn't expect to ever return to school but I knew that I couldn't look back.

I was so close to those doors. So close to pushing my way out into the cold sunlight. That's when I heard Hailey.

"Kaya!". Her voice rang clear through the hallway. It was as if her voice was a sharp knife, cutting through the conversations and laughter of the people surrounding us. It's weird how I remember details; I bit my lip and closed my eyes. The guy pushing past me was wearing neon green sneakers. I knew I had to turn around. I couldn't offend her even though it felt like it would take all I had left. Pausing for what felt like hours, I finally turned around. Hailey was too far away for me to see while I kept my eyes on the ground.

And despite avoiding any eye contact for the past weeks; despite knowing that it would rip my heart in two—or maybe exactly because I knew that would happen and I needed a final push—I slowly met her gaze. Her amber eyes bore into mine. I saw love, but also concern. I was able to read so much more in them than I wanted to. Love, worry, sadness, fear, suspicion, a trace of annoyance … Some images just stay with you. That is one of them.

I wanted to go up and hug her. I wanted it so bad I felt like I was going to collapse right there on the floor if I wasn't able to breathe in her Hailey scent and feel her familiar embrace. But at the same time I was afraid of it. Afraid of feeling the comfort. Scared of how much she'd be able to notice once she held me close. Terrified of my façade crumbling down around us. I looked over my shoulder; the double doors were close. Just a few steps away. Easy.

Dragging my eyes back to my best friend, I gave her a small wave. I even tried to smile but I still don't know if I succeeded. This is how she'd last seen me—that was one of my final thoughts before passing out later that day. A small wave after all these years.

I couldn't bear to wait for a reaction, so I turned around towards those doors. And that's when I realized I was wrong: the doors were not the easier way, nor closer. It was hard to get there, and every step seemed to carry me further away from where I wanted to be.

"Baby, it's ok. It's ok. Tell me what's wrong. Honey, what is it?" She puts her hands on either side of my face, forcing me to look at her. I can tell she is trying to find out what it is. What it is that is bothering me. And why I'm standing in the middle of Fashion Valley crying countless tears.

"Nothing, I'm fine. I'm fine." I snort because I'm still sobbing and it's just so far from the truth. And we both know it.

She looks at me, her face serious. I avoid her eyes and let a curtain of hair fall between us. Wiping my tears with my fingers, I brace myself for what she is going to say next. It only takes a peak for me to know that what she is going to say will be uncomfortable. Her mouth opens, yet I see the hesitation in her eyes.

The tension is broken by a shrill ringing. I jump and blush, feeling silly for letting her ringtone scare me. Hailey's eyes linger on me for another moment while she fishes her iPhone out of her bag.

"Hello? Ok, we're coming." She ends the phone call.

"Our parents are waiting for us." And though she looks like she might say something else, she simply steps back and links her arm through mine.

14

"Did you have a nice time with Hailey?" My mom tries to sound casual, but I know better. She sees it as a big step that I met up with my friend again. She is afraid it might have overwhelmed me. She is worried Hailey may have asked or said something that could have upset me. She is terrified that all these months of therapy will disappear because of a spur of the moment comment by Hailey or someone else in the mall. She is concerned that seeing all those clothes will make me want to control my diet again.

None of this has ever been directly said to me, but that's the thing between mom and me: she thinks she knows me so well, but she has no idea just how see-through she is to me.

Looking at my mother nowadays scares me. She used to be this strong, independent woman. She was my rock, even if she may not have known this. I felt like she could make everything better, no matter what was wrong. Since I was a young girl I always had her as my support. I fought against her, defied her and pretended that she was way off and completely wrong. Especially in later years. But deep down I always knew she was—mostly—right. Guess that's just a mom thing; they just have it all figured out somehow. Or they can make you believe they do.

Even if her world was in crumbles, she seemed to know how to handle mine.

I never saw my mom cry. Or my dad, for that matter. But lately it seems it's been all she's been doing. As if it's my fault. Well, I guess it kind of is. I did pick up that knife and make her worry ever since. But I didn't mean to ruin her life. Never was that my intention. I kind of almost thought I'd do her, well maybe not a favour, but something good. Instead, I only complicated her life. Made her miserable and hopeless. I made her feel little and small and unimportant. As if I barely cared—I'm self-ish, but she didn't want to realize that and always hoped I was different. Typical sweet mother instinct. And then she got angry when she saw a glimpse of my real self; the selfish one. The one that only used her for its own bene-fit, but wouldn't even take her advice. We've yelled about it enough times so I know it's true. But that was before. Now we don't yell. Only soft voices; she doesn't want to upset me. And it's my fault. Everything is my fault.

"Ya, I did." I beam at mom. Running my fingers through my hair I shrug my shoulder and try to look cute and naïve. Believable, I guess. Because it is true. And yet I feel like I need to prove it. Everything seems like a scene from a play. Some people say that life's a stage, but I'm tired of it. I used to be good at it and now apparently I'm not, because I can't even make the truth believable. People constantly told me how happy I always am and how good I am at everything I do, but they never realized that I was a damn good actress too. And now it's all gone. I've got nothing left.

"We went to MAC and got smoothies and it was so nice to laugh with her and see her, and just have Hailey be Hailey and …" I babble on, filling the silence with the oh-so unbelievable truth that my mom will never buy again.

> Hey stranger
>
> Oh sure, now you've got time for me
>
> Haha, sorry … still not over it?
>
> Getting there
>
> Good!
>
> How was your girl-time?
>
> Long needed.
>
> Glad you had fun
>
> I did, actually.
>
> Seem surprized
>
> Ya, guess I am. It's been a while
>
> For you and Hailey?
>
> For me and a lot of people.
>
> Hm … ok.
>
> What?
>
> I like that about you
>
> What … my good-looks? ;)
>
> Hahaha, nooo … well, yes, but not what I meant ;)
>
> Hahaha I'm flattered.

Sitting in my room I'm staring at my desk. My English book is lying in front of me, but I haven't even cracked the cover yet. I'm afraid of what I'll find inside. I'm even scared of googling a synopsis because then I know how it ends. And I don't want to. I don't want to know how Callie's story ends. What if it's negative and I have to give up all my hope for my own happy ending? Then again, as depressing as this book might be, I doubt it's going to be a suicide story. That wouldn't exactly be a class literature kind of thing. Incredible how one book has managed to kill my "I love English class so much" buzz. But I have to read it. I want a good grade. And I need to be prepared.

I can't walk into that class again and be taken off guard. I've seen the looks over the past few days. The whispers, the stares. Fair enough, they have reduced themselves from the hallways to my reading group. But still. It's not like they have stopped. I merely choose to ignore them. Or, pretend I do. More acting. Life's a stage, baby.

Gosh, how I hate that book. Kind of funny in a way. I believe in fate from time to time. Like, I'm convinced of love at first sight (though it hasn't happened to me so far). I also believe in people having destinies sometimes. Things they are born to do or to preach. Gandhi, for example. I highly doubt he woke up one morning and just decided to fight for rights. Well, maybe he did, but it was pre-decided. It was his destiny, which is more or less the same as fate.

But this; no, this can't be fate. What on earth would the purpose of it be? It's a coincidence, that's all. True, quite a big coincidence that after being absent for attempting suicide and being in treatment for months, this book is not only being read in my class by one of the groups, but by my group. But coincidences happen. You forget your iPod on the bus and your best friend happens to hop on at the next stop, recognizing it as yours and returns it to you safely the next day. (Again, this hasn't happened to me.)

My point is that this is just a really stupid coincidence. And I just have to live with it and tough it out. It's a book—what harm could come from reading it?

I take a deep breath and open "Cut" to the first page.

15

"Kaya." My mother's voice is slowly coming through to me through the wall I always build around myself when reading. In the past two hours I relocated myself to my bed, where I continued reading propped up against my purple pillows that always cover my day spread. It always happens this way; I lose myself in the world the author creates no matter how terrible the writing may be. I get absorbed in it. I breathe the emotions and see the character. It's like a movie in my head. It's the reason I love English Lit so much. Until this book came along, that is.

I snap out of my bubble when I hear her brusque rapping on the door. I have just enough time to slide the book under my pillow when she opens the door. No way will I tell her about that book.

"What are you doing?" Her suspicious gaze travels over me and my bed. She is clearly trying to detect the activity I must have been up to. I can tell from the suspicious/worried/upset/guarded/sharp/hopeful look she is giving me that she fears my answer. Or the lie behind it because that is all she will see no matter how honest I might be.

"Daydreaming." I smile at her reassuringly. She hesitates for a split second; long enough for me to see nevertheless. But whatever is on her mind, she doesn't push it.

"Do you want to go to Café Chloé? Your dad will be working late tonight, so I thought we could have a girl dinner." I nod instantly, excited at the prospect of going back there.

"Meet you at the car in 10?"

Café Chloé is definitely one of my favourite places to eat. It's so charming and French. Though, let's be honest, I highly doubt any French person would feel at home here, but whatever. The chairs are iron carved and the front room is flooded with light. All the tables are quite small, usually for not more than maximum three people. The decoration is simple, dark and purple mainly like the restaurant's logo. It has so much charm, and the food is amazing. The portions are quite small, but they make delicious fruit tarts of various kinds.

Mom and I sit at a table at the window. Despite it being fall already, the temperatures are still high and the air con is my best friend on days like these.

I enjoy sitting here, sipping my lavender lemonade and observing the people around us. There's the typical middle-aged couple where the wife had way too many appointments with the beauty Doc and the husband simply couldn't care less because he is too glued to his smartphone to even realize. Then we've got that young couple that is so lovey-dovey and basically devouring each other with their eyes, living in their own bubble of happiness. The young woman with her red curls pinned up who is reading a book while absentmindedly attracting the attention of a boy, I'm guessing slightly older than me, who is having a family dinner. His folks seem like the kind of parents who take their offspring on long journeys all across the world and solve crosswords at the breakfast table. They have a little girl with them as well, about nine, in a frilly princess dress. I smile. I used to have a dress just like it. When I was a young girl, frilly dresses were all I'd wear. I loved the way they'd swish around my legs when I was twirling round and round. They made me feel like a princess. Like all those Disney princesses form my favourite movies. I used to even have the costumes from them; Halloween may be the festival of scary creatures and horror for some, but it always gave me the chance to dress up like one of the characters from Disney. One year I was the little mermaid with a bright red wig and a shiny fishtail. A year later I was Snow White, while my mom played the evil witch. My favourite costume of all though was that of Jasmine. Aladdin was—and I admit, sometimes still is—my absolute favourite movie. There, Jasmine is the princess and Aladdin needs saving, not the other way around. And the whole scenery is so pretty and enchanting and Abbu the cutest monkey ever.

"What are you thinking about?" I am startled by my mom's voice. She follows my gaze to the little girl who is now tugging at her brother's hand, trying to get him to entertain her.

"You used to have a dress just like that."

"That's what I was just thinking about. Disney were my absolute favourite movies." We smile at each other, both of us reminiscing about the past. Things were easy back then. I smiled and meant it. Of course I did; I was seven.

Being a little kid is amazing. The world is at your feet and you can dream and have hopes. Everything seems possible. One moment you're absolutely convinced you want to become a princess. The next you decide that being a horse back rider is the way to go. Or maybe a lawyer is better and more suitable. Depending on what age I was, my ideal dream job changed. My friends influenced me; their dreams gave me new ideas and inspired them. Back and forth, like on a seesaw. Always keeping an eye on each other; gauging the other person's reaction and adapting your moves accordingly.

"So how is school going, honey?"

"It's good." Silence. Not good. "It's quite easy to keep up with work, even though I've … you know, been gone for a bit." Silence again. Damn, I need to think quickly.

"Easy?" She beats me to it.

"Well, ya. I mean … I'm not too stupid, you know." She gives me a look. It's an uncomfortable look, but I choose to ignore it.

"I know, honey, I never said that. I just mean you haven't been working so much lately. I haven't seen you study. But if you're keeping up, well, I'm glad. Just … try not to fall behind."

"I'm not falling behind. Didn't you just hear me? I'm keeping up just fine."

"I know, sweety, I know. I'm just saying. For your whole academic life."

"Uhu." I stare into my purple drink. Heat is boiling up inside of me; hot, white and fast. She always does this. Critizises me without trying. I swallow empty, fighting the urge to explode. I'm good at school. She doesn't mean it that way. I don't have to be perfect. I'm good at school. She doesn't mean it that way. I don't have to be flawless; I'm perfect the way I am. I repeat it in my head like a mantra. It's hard to push away the feelings that are washing over me, threatening to drown me. I don't want that again; I'm done with hating my-self, with being worthless. I don't have to be flawless; I'm perfect the way I am. As if.

Closing the door behind me, I lean against it. I try to steady my breathing. There it is. On my bed, where I left it. With every passing second I spend staring at it, it seems to grow. Becoming larger, soaking up the oxygen in the room. My breathing turns shallow. I need to start writing my report.

With my eyes on the book like a suspect at the CIA, I fire up my laptop. Anxiety waves wash over me. I'm not the biggest fan of school in general, but this report is the worst. I've never hated an assignment so passionately.

Even the thought of it closes my throat and makes me feel like I'm suffocating. I feel the need to gasp for air and to swallow; survival instincts. Breathe, Kaya, breathe. I open up my email and check what the group assigned for me. Kaya—summary & character depiction—include motivations/development. I can do that. That's easy and detached. I can work with that. I open a few browsers and hesitantly grab my copy of the book.

A summer is quickly done. I paraphrase a mix of a few I find on the internet and then add in parts I find important. This is not too difficult, not too allconsuming. It's words and text and moments that I just need to put into a linear order. A puzzle, in a way. Before I know it, I'm done. A nice 250 word summary is staring back at me from my computer screen.

Next task; characters. Callie first. And the hardest. She is the main character, that part is easy. And she develops from someone who doesn't say a word in therapy, to someone who actively wants to get better. And this is where it gets tricky. Because the lines between fiction included in the book and the reality that I'm living is suddenly very blurry. It's not nearly as clear cut as it should be. Books are supposed to be able to transport you into that world they're describing. You are supposed to feel the characters' emotions. Despair, love, hope, joy—it's all the same and it's all meant to be yours as well. And in this book it is. Scarily so. I know how relieved Callie must feel when she is able to break that aluminium plate in half and put one of the slices in her pocket. The feeling of security and serenity that washes over her. She knows she'll be ok because she has what she needs. Even if she doesn't use it right now, it's there. She can touch it through the fabric of her jeans. It's like a shield protecting her from numbness. It's the way I've felt so many times. Just knowing that a scissor or knife will be waiting for me when I get home is not always enough. Sometimes I needed reassurance right there and then. A scissor in my pencil case. A loose nail that broke off. A knife at lunch, easy to slide into your bag. Anything I can hold onto. I know how she feels.

And I understand exactly the urge to cut. The point where you're so close to combusting that you need to let the tension out. And because you're so numb you want to feel alive and hence hurt yourself, to remind yourself that though you are dying inside your body is still alive.

Except that Callie experiences something I never have. I've never known how it is to cut, to see the blood, to have the tension nearly rip you apart—and then feel pain. Not delicious, sweet pain. But the bad kind. A dull throbbing that pulses through your veins and heart and hurts in your ears. The kind that comes from an accident or anything unintentional. The physical kind you never want to feel.

That part of the story fascinated me. The way she described it. How she didn't feel relief, even though she expected to. The concept is foreign to me. Even that one time I did it during my stay at the clinic, it still felt good. I knew it was bad, I knew that technically I shouldn't be enjoying it. But it felt incredible. It was like what being high must feel like.

What drives Callie? What drives all of us? Survival instincts. It's a way to feel and know and show yourself that you're still alive. She never tries to kill herself. So her cutting is probably driven by her need to be alive. Relief from what's suffocating her. Punishment because she is not doing everything right. Then again, who is?

16

"Don't crack." For a moment I fold my hands over his to keep him from doing it. Just as fast I withdraw my hands, but the feel of his warm skin burns into my palms. Tim looks down at me with a twinkle in his eyes, oblivious to the fire in my hand.

"Pet peeve of yours?"

"My worst. I hate it. A lot." He grins at me. I can't mind-read, but I'm pretty sure I know what he intends to do.

"No. No, no, no, no!" Pushing my chair away from him I cover my ears. No use. The crack pierces through my body. I hate that sound so much. Chalk on a blackboard or even nails, with that I can deal, no problem. Knuckle cracking—no way in hell.

"Stop." Crack.

"Come on, I beg you!" He grins devilishly. The twinkle in his eyes becomes amplified. Two little horns are starting to form on his head and a pointed tail from his back. His teeth become razor sharp in my imagination and his smile creepily wide.

"Beg?" Devil Tim grins even more wickedly.

"Yes, begging."

"Doesn't sound like it just yet."

"Beg, beg, beg, beg …" He laughs and it warms my

heart. The sound is so carefree and honest that the devil image melts away and Tim is back. Smiling, sweet. And still intent on cracking his stupid knuckles.

"Nice try." He winks and then pulls his finger, creating the most horrendous snapping/cracking sound. People around us look up from their conversations to pinpoint the source of that noise.

"Idiot!" I slap his arm only half playfully. He yowls in fake pain and throws himself onto the floor, clutching his arm. I try hard to fight my smile, but it's difficult. He looks pretty cute lying on the floor like that, completely overreacting. Isn't there this rule or something: When a guy tries to make you laugh, he likes you? No, it's probably something else.

"Oh no! Are you ok?" My voice doesn't sound half as concerned as I'd like it to because I'm trying to choke back my giggle. He is rolling around on the floor grunting and yelping as if he was shot or otherwise seriously injured. Not too bad an actor, that boy.

"Mr. Weaver, it pains me too that I was held up in a meeting, but this is a slight overreaction for a mere five minutes, wouldn't you agree?" The room has gone completely quiet. As cliché as it may be, one could probably hear a pin drop.

"Absolutely, Mr. Tanner. Won't happen again."

"I have no doubts about that. At all." While our teacher places his file on the desk and starts rummaging through it for his lesson plan, Tim takes a seat next to me.

"All for you, baby." He winks and I smile.

"Lunch?"

"Sure." I smile up at him while I get up and collect my books.

"Mind if I stop by my locker? I hate carrying all these books with me." He gives me a look.

"What?" Another look.

"What is it?" Tim raises his eyebrows.

"Come on, tell me!"

"I'm pretty sure shortly after we met we had an incident from which was established that you really should carry a bag with you. Daily."

"Hey! I do. Well, almost daily. Oh just shut up. And stop looking at me like that!" He rolls his eyes at me.

"Ok it'll make me look like a 5 year old but …" I stick out my tongue at him. He laughs and I feel as if something flutters in my stomach. Must be my skipping breakfast. Most important meal of the day, definitely shouldn't make a habit out of it. Not that I ever could, the way my mom watches over me. Today was only possible because I was seriously late for school and mom was at the grocery store.

"I shouldn't encourage your resistance to bags but I can't bear seeing you struggle with your stuff …" I grin and before he knows it, I'm shoving everything into his arms. He laughs at me.

"Not what I meant."

"Would a gentleman really refuse a lady's wishes?" He grins cheekily.

"Who said that I'm a gentleman?" He winks at me. Continuing in this joking manner, we're at my locker before I even realize it. People are pushing past us, but the proximity of the hallway doesn't get to me today. For some reason, it's ok. I'm ok.

I'm shoving my books into my locker, listening to his voice. It's louder than everyone else's, though not in an uncomfortable way. I'd use the words piercing, but that is negative. His voice isn't. It's just as if everyone else fades into the background. Guess it just never occurred to me that he speaks this loudly. I just wasn't really paying attention, I suppose. But it's nice being able to focus on one voice, one story only. I hate it when the halls are so crowded and you hear snippets of other people's conversations. Conversations you are not a part of, that have nothing to do with you and yet you know a little bit about someone else's life or thoughts or opinions. I always wonder how much others have learnt about me this way. Do they know who my best friend is?

Have they figured out that I was absent for months? Maybe some random people on the street have heard fragments of my conversations and were able to see through all the bullshit and went home to their families and told them about a girl they had seen whose life was falling apart and who couldn't even deal with herself. And in the meantime my friends simply saw the smile, the lies.

Sometimes it's easier to see through the façade when you're not on the inside of the bubble. Some people see right to the bottom of things, even if they can't explain why. Would I maybe have been ok if one of those people had spoken up? If just one person had asked: "Are you ok? You need help."

Feeling lonely when you're alone, well, it hurts. Being plunged into darkness at night scares you, but it's hard to tell the difference between the inside and the out. But feeling lonely amongst a crowd of people and being surrounded by darkness in the sunshine—that's the worst kind of pain. It's like that first moment when your skin touches boiling water and it feels cold. For just a split second the burning liquid freezes you. And then it burns. This is the same, but worse. Freezing or burning implies that I feel something, even pain. But I don't. I'd scream, but I am just this hollow shell. Wrapped up in darkness so tightly that sounds and noises are heard to hear. I'm trying to concentrate, but the world keeps slipping from me. When my friends laugh, so do I. I even speak. I don't know where the words are coming from, but it doesn't matter. Nothing does. My silent scream reverberates through my empty insides like an echo in a pitch-black cave. The contrast between the vivid world I'm in and the way I feel; it's not even comparable. An overwhelming feeling of being behind a one-sided glass wall grips me. I can see them, but I'm invisible. If only it were so easy. If only disappearing could be that simple.

"Kaya? Earth to Kaya." Tim waves his hand in front of my face and it takes me a second to reorientate myself.

"I'm sorry, I just totally spaced out."
"You do that a lot, don't you." It's not really a question, more of a statement. An uncomfortable feeling starts spreading in my stomach. He noticed. My façade is crumbling. I need to be more careful. I don't want him to know why I space out. That sometimes little things just hit me and my thoughts race away before I even realize it. Memories flood me and I'm drowning in the past.

"I'm just kind of a dreamer, I guess. Nothing personal. "Tim studies me with his blue eyes, today the colour of ice. Then he slowly nods.

"Dreaming is good, it's what makes things happen." If only you knew, I think.

"Ya, I guess it does. So what is your dream?"

"If you tell a dream, it won't come true."

"That's shooting stars."

"That's my theory."

"No disrespect, but your theory sucks." He stares at me in fake hurt as he holds the cafeteria door open for me.
"This is your way of trying to convince me to tell you about my dreams?"

"If you put it that way … please?" I stare up at him from under my lashes, trying to imitate a puppy dog look. I bite my lip and brush a strand of hair behind my ear. A look fleets across his face. I can't quite determine it but, for just a second his eyes flick away from my face nervously. Then suddenly he regains control of his emotions. He settles on amused.

"Well now you really aren't playing fair. How could I ever resist that cute puppy dog look?"

"Then don't. So what are your dreams?" I reach for a chocolate mousse, but hesitate, pulling my hand back. Then I reach for it again, still unsure. Maybe better not. I'm gaining too much weight anyway. I mean, that's what people looking at me must be thinking. God is she a fattie.

Tim grabs the chocolate mousse and places it on my tray, before taking his own. I look up at him, baffled.

"Chocolate's good for the soul. Anyway, I dream of a lot of things. Stuff, normal things."

"Still not an answer."

"The best answer I can give you."

"Ok, fine, then my next question. What's your goal?" He smirks.

"Same thing, baby, same thing." We walk to a table in silence, while I contemplate this. Tim is seriously not going to confide in me. It's just dreams. We all have them. Goals, hope … it's human. Then again, would I want to bare my soul? Would I want to tell him what I dreamt of every day while sitting in therapy with some person who tries to pry answers out of me by manipulating my emotions?

"Fair enough."

"So what do you dream of? What's your goal?" I look up from my food and meet his eyes. He seems genuinely curious. His gaze is open and friendly. Shall I tell him? With other people the answer would be clear: no. Because they would never understand. They'd judge. They'd just want to hear the good things. College, dream job, white picket fence. Not the truth that lies behind my smile.

I look down at my plate and shake my head slightly. Being normal is exhausting.

"We all have a story, you know. I'm here for you, just so you know." The serious tone of his voice surprises me and I glance up at him through my lashes. I try to smile but I can't. He is compelling me, his eyes piercing right through me. I suddenly feel stripped off everything. Every fake laugh and smile, every 'I'm fine' that I've ever uttered. My heart is picking up speed, tripping and stumbling while I'm trying not to shake. I'm afraid of what he is reading in my eyes, of what he is seeing behind my soul. He claims he'll be there for me, but he can't know. He just can't. Because he wouldn't be. My parents can barely deal with it. So why should he be any different? Someone I've known only for a few weeks. He'll be more terrified than anyone. He'll never understand.

"I'm sorry." I mumble the words over my shoulder as I dash away, out of the cafeteria and down the hall until —once again—I'm leaning against the cool wall in the last stall in the girls' bathroom. Alone, again.

"Hey, wait up." Somebody grabs my arm in the hallway. I hate this time of day—the after school rush when everybody is trying to get out as quick as they can. It's crowded and loud and confusing. I yank my arm away before spinning around to whoever grabbed me. My heart is racing a little from the closeness. I hate physical contact.

It's Angela, the girl with the fiery red hair from my English group. My smile slips from my face and I scowl at her. Excuse me for not forgiving her those very rude comments.

"What?"

"Catty, much? I just wanted to tell you that we are meeting at lunch tomorrow to go over our parts of the presentation. To practice the whole thing and stuff. That cool with you?" She raises her eyebrows so arrogantly that my palm is twitching to smack the expression off her face.

"Ya, sure. We have to do it at some point." She stares at me for a moment before nodding and wordlessly walking the other way. So much for rudeness.

17

I'm standing outside the classroom, pressed against the wall. Breathe, Kaya, breathe. The voices inside are loud and dominant. I don't like Angela's. It's too high pitched and arrogant and rude and snotty and just plain annoying. The other girl, Jessica I found out, is barely audible. Her voice is usually more of a breathy whisper, especially compared to the red-head's. My notes, laptop and book are in my arms and I'm hugging them tightly. I can feel the tension in my shoulders. My knuckles are white from the pressure of my grip. A slightly metallic taste is in my mouth and I release my lower lip from between my teeth. You can do this.

Heavy footsteps make me stand up straighter and turn my head slightly, enough so that I'm able to glance down the row of lockers. John is approaching swiftly, obviously in a hurry.

"Sorry sorry sorry, I know I'm late."

"No worries." I flash him my best I'm-totally-ok-don't-worry-about-me smile. He smiles back; simple and honest, not hard to decipher.

"How come you're lounging out here?" Oh shit. Think, Kaya, think. I lean in closer and whisper.

"Angela." He rolls his eyes knowingly.

"I feel you. Come on, let's get this over with." Nodding, I walk into the classroom behind him. Too late to run now.

"Finally", Angela hisses, glaring first at John and then at me.

"We're here now, aren't we?" John isn't even remotely intimidated by her and I'm glad for his presence. I knew a friendship was under way.

"Whatever. Let's get started. So, John, what have you come up with?" He opens up his laptop and clicks us through a few slides while explaining what he will say and how he imagines it should all flow into each other. I nod along with the others, listening to him talk about the author and her intentions and reasons for writing this novel. His choice of words makes it clear that he has a large vocabulary and I like the perspective he is taking.

"I don't know, seems a little … I don't know, out of the blue." Angela purses her lips and rapidly clicks through John's slides. He rolls his eyes and shakes his head slightly, clearly exasperated at her. I get it; his slides are brilliant; his approach to the author interesting and original—she should just let it be.

"I think it's good." Jessica's voice is so shaky that I can barely hear her. Angela does; she silences her with a look, cold enough to freeze an ocean.

"I'm just saying, I think it doesn't have the effect."

"Shut up, Angela. It's good, let it be." Everyone turns to me and even I am surprised at my own outburst. The red-head squints at me, fury evident in her eyes. Definitely didn't make myself a friend in her.

"Thanks, Kaya. Up top." John stretches out to give me a high five and though I know in my gut that it's just a slap in Angela's face, I meet his palm midair.

Angela is quiet for the rest of the meeting, more focused on staring me down and making me squirm than anything. I have a bad feeling about this. Even though I enjoy having John integrate me so naturally, she kind of scares me. So when the bell signalling the end of lunch goes off, I hang around the room, watching her gather her stuff. The other two have already left for their classes and it won't be long before other students come ready for 5th period. Taking a deep breath, I approach her.

"Hey, look, about earlier …"

"Not interested", she cuts me off, whipping her fiery hair back like a burning mane.

"I'm just trying to say that …"

"Save it, Kaya. You think you can come waltzing in here, put me down in order to flirt with John, and get away with it?" She takes a step closer to me and suddenly I'm scared. She is so close I can smell her perfume, something rich and smothering.

"I see how you flinch whenever we bring up Callie's self-harm. I saw the look on your face during English Lit when you were assigned this book. True, the whispers died down, but it won't take a lot to fuel them again." I see my face reflected in her dark eyes. My expression is impassive, thank god, but I can see a flicker in my eyes. I'm praying she doesn't, but I just can't be sure. She clearly knows more than she has let on. I take a big step back.

"I have genuinely no clue what you are referring to. I just can't believe we are reading such a pathetic book in English Lit when we could be discussing the Brontes. And really, save the empty threats. I want a good grade as badly as you do, so let's just get through this and then we never have to speak to each other again unless absolutely necessary." My heart is racing and I hear the pounding of my blood in my own ears. I hope my words sound more confident and honest than I feel. She can't know. She just cannot know. And I just can't let her see.

"I'll see you later", I say over my shoulder before heading out the door, eager to escape her. I don't look back, but I swear I can feel her eyes piercing through me all the way out the door and down the hallway.

"Honey, you should eat some more. Your plate is still almost full." My mom is nervously fiddling with her napkin, smiling at me.

"I'm good, mom."

"Well, but darling, maybe some more sauce?"

"Mom, drop it. I'm full." Now her smile slips. She breathes deeply and gives dad a pointed look. He gives her one back. Subtle, people, real subtle.

"So, Kaya, how is it going in school? Still good to be back?

"With mom, this question would make me cringe and

make me take a deep breath; with dad, on the other hand, it's somehow ok. He is not looking for more than a conversation. He just takes me at face-value and understands that I've got to live in the moment rather than be dragging my issues with me through life.

"It's good, actually. I really enjoy it. Good hanging out with Hailey again; I really missed her."

"Well, of course you did after such a long time." My mom winces and I can't be sure, but I have a sneaky feeling that dad may have kicked her a bit underneath the table. To please her and to hide my smile, I take another bite of my pasta. I really am full. She needs to lay off. I was there when the doctors said that I was anorexic and underweight. I was there when my parents were told to make sure I'd eat every single meal for the next few weeks. I was there when Victoria, the sweet nurse from the hospital, comforted me because I cried when she made me eat my food. I was there, mom. I get it.

"I can imagine. She is great. Feel free to bring her around any time."

"Thanks, daddy."

"Anything for you, kiddo. Now go do your homework!" He winks at me, but I know he means it as well.

"I don't have a lot to do." My parents exchange a look.

"I'm sure there is lots for you to revise. For finals, for example. Or just go over the things you did in class." My mom's voice is still calm, but I hear the urgency. I clench my fist under the table.

"Finals are far away and I have caught up, mom. Leave it up to me."

"Honey, I just don't want you to fall behind."

"I won't." She throws my dad a pleading look. This is pointless; he is going to take her side. It's a stupid parent thing. They always take each other's sides against mine. I'm always alone.

"Baby girl, then work ahead. Make us proud." He smiles at me. I fake it back.

"Of course, daddy." I can't win. Make them proud—I have heard it before. They demand and want and ask for things, but in front of others they say how proud they are and how amazingly well I am doing. Sometimes they will even tell me to my face; I hate that even more. They say they are proud and that I am so good at what I do and so forth, yet they always want to tell me how to live my life and how there is so much more work I could be doing.

I grab our plates and stack them to carry them to the kitchen counter. I wordlessly put all the cutlery and the glasses and our plates into the dishwasher, listening to my parent's talk to each other. This is how it's supposed to be; a normal family unit without any pressure to be perfect or to act a certain way.

"I'm gonna go upstairs." I kiss my dad on the cheek and after a second of hesitation do the same with my mom.

"Sure. Have fun. Don't climb out of your window." I smack him on the arm.

"Damn, how did you know?"

Math is certainly not my thing. And it's quite depressing. Not in that way, I'm not that instable, but in the sense of that it's irritating and demotivating because I used to be so good at it. My mom would probably blame my absence from school for this, but my difficulties with math set in much earlier. I just can't seem to handle it. That was always one of the most difficult things about my depression—my actual one. It all accumulated. My low mood made me bored and lazy, and I couldn't make myself work. That's the part my mom, and even my dad, just don't understand. It wasn't that I was demotivated—I just literally could not make myself work. My mind drifted, I was tired, confused, had to read questions over and over before even a slight meaning sunk in. Studying was the hardest. I could stare at a passage for hours and I still wouldn't be able to tell you what it was about. My mind was blank. And probably the worst part was that I didn't even care. When I got a D in an exam I wasn't just acting like it didn't affect me, because it genuinely didn't. I knew rationally that I should be upset, but I couldn't be. I couldn't feel. My bad grades made my parents complain. They told me I should try harder. I felt guilty. I felt dumb. I felt useless and worthless. I spiralled further because I already knew this. I was fat and ugly and stupid and not worth anything. I even felt bad for wasting my parents' time on me. I felt bad about everything; after all, it was all my fault. Story of my life.

Now, 8 months later I've barely come anywhere. It's still my fault; that my parents worry, that I'm bad at math, that I cost them so much money for my therapy and all. And it's not even helping.

That's probably the worst part. Sometimes I really do feel like I'm better. Like joking with my dad at dinner. I felt good, normal. But it's the exception. Letting myself feel is still so hard for me. It's easier and seems more natural to my nature to suppress my feelings and fake what I think people want to see. I can't talk to Theresa about it. Yes, she has helped me. All of it has. I don't feel that ugly anymore and I'm eating. I even let myself have treats and I don't feel guilty. So I guess that's a success. But can it really cancel out the urges I still get? The need to take something sharp and to make myself feel better. The moment of anticipation, the moment of quick, sharp pain—the sign that I'm still alive and that I can feel.

A sudden chime from my cell makes me jump. I'm thankful to be ripped out of my daydream. The direction it was headed in is a dangerous one. Better focus on simple, normal things.

I check my phone; it's a whatsapp from Tim. And even though it's totally random and makes absolutely no sense, I smile.

> **Hey! What's up?**
>
> **Hi! Not much. Math. U?**
>
> **Nothing. Physics.**
>
> **Fun times**
>
> **You know it**

I hate these type of conversations. When you just don't
know what to say. When you want to keep talking to the
person, but everything that pops to mind seems phony
and pathetic. Not that it would matter; I'm not trying
to impress him. But even my friends shouldn't think of
me as a bad texter.

> So … how's life?
> Deep, deep. It's good. U?
>
> Confusing, irritating, hard.
>
> Same here. Btw … wanna have lunch tomorrow? I
> don't feel like typing – too exhausting ;
> Haha. Yeah, sure. I'll pick u up from bio :p
> Lol, perfect. G'night :* <3
> Good night :* <3

I bite my lip, proud and surprised at myself. We've never
had lunch. We've texted, sure. And we've talked in class
and between classes and stuff. And obviously we've eaten
together at the same table with lots of people. But never
just him and me. Wait, what if he misunderstood me?
No, he's smart, I'm sure he got what I meant. But what
if he didn't? I'd just have to go along with it. We could
always have lunch another day, no biggie.

Oh my gosh, I'm having lunch with Tim. Not that it matters, we're just friends. But I still want him to like me. I mean, he hopefully does; we do text and are friends after all.

I get up and open my closet, casually looking through my clothes. No reason, just feel like planning my outfit for tomorrow. Then I don't have to do it in the morning and it'll save me some time. So I can sleep longer or something. Sleep is important. Sleep is vital.

"Hey, babe. You look nice. Love the shoes." Ruby glances at my feet enviously, before smiling at me.

"Thanks, doll. I love your handbag." She pretends to be surprised though it's clear she wants everyone to notice the big brand engraved on the front of it.

"Oh, thanks. You're so sweet. My mom got it for me from Boston. God, I really miss home." And I know that this she does mean. Ruby and I met in Junior High, a year after she had moved all across the country from Boston to San Diego because of her dad's job. It was pretty evident that she was not from around here. Nothing against dolling up, but her style was so obviously New Yorkesque, it was quite unique. And here we are, three years later, and Ruby looks exactly the same, acts exactly the same and is exactly as fake. Sometimes I really wonder why we are friends.

"Wanna grab sushi tonight? Hailey and Emily are totally up for it." Now I remember. We often have loads of fun together, especially on sushi nights. Only now does it strike me that I haven't been on a single one since I came back. They are our tradition; every Thursday night we go to our local sushi restaurant. We bonded that way years ago and it kind of just stuck.

"Hell ya. Can't wait." I beam at her and she returns the favour cheerfully.

"Yay, see you then."

"You sure will." She blows me a kiss before disappearing in the crowd, head held high, bag carried proud.

"Yay." I roll my eyes at Tim's pathetic imitation of my friend.

"Come on, she ain't that bad."

"Never said she was."

"Not verbally, but texting."

"What's said in text, stays in text." I smack his arm and start walking towards Biology.

"Oh come on, you yourself said that she acts fake."

"I know I did and she does, but we are still friends. And besides, you're her friend too."

"No. I just pretend I am."

"Then you are no better than her."

"Maybe I learned from the best." I decide to not argue his point since he'd just have a comeback anyway. It's something I've learned to really love about Tim in the past few weeks. He is so witty and clever; he doesn't back down when I tease him. In fact, he'll do it right back.

"We still on for lunch?" I just keep walking to our seats, hoping he can't see my joy that he remembered.

"Sure. How could we not?"

18

"You do know that people are staring, right?" Tim smiles at me and I give him credit for not turning around to glance over his shoulder to our usual table. It's ridiculous how our friends are not even trying to hide their curiosity. They talk, stare and even point. And I have a sneaky feeling that they are not the only ones. It's the way it always was. As soon as two people from the opposite sex start spending time together, people talk. It's dumb and silly, because hello, you can just be friends. So everyone should just cut it out and mind their own business.

"I know. So? Do you care?"

"No." Yes. I don't want people to stare. I want to be close to invisible; invisible, unseen, not attracting attention and safe.

"Do you?"

"No. We can be friends, right? Who cares what they think." I don't know if it's his warm smile or his clear blue eyes, but I find myself agreeing. Who cares? We know and that's enough.

"Can I ask you something?" Suddenly he seems almost tangibly nervous. I can't quite pinpoint what it is that gives me that impression—his face is still impassive, and he isn't fiddling either, just calmly eating his food. But for some reason I feel this tension oozing from him; whether it's his hand on the fork that's just a little bit tense or something in his deep, guarded eyes. My hands grow just the slightest bit colder and I supress a shiver. Questions are never good. They lead to inquiries and those lead to investigations and answers. I don't want to answer.

The noise around us seems to quiet down and then gradually disappear. I'm focusing on him alone; the curve of his jaw, the slant of his eyebrows. The movement of his lips as he is forming his words. His lips look soft and relaxed and for just a spilt second I wonder what it's like to kiss him. Hormones, seriously. And then the moment has passed and I zone in on his question.

"Can I?"

"You just did, didn't you."

"I mean another one."

"Go ahead." He hesitates and I hold my breath. Then I force it out between tight lips. It's nothing, I'm sure the question is completely harmless.

"Why were you gone so long?" No. No, no, no, no.

"What do you mean?"

"Last year … I heard, you know, that you were in Switzerland at your aunt's. You just kind of take off without a warning." I can't believe it. My bubble just burst. He knows. And he thinks I'm a freak. Oh gosh, does he know it all? Does everyone? No. It's just rumours. Unrelated and stupid. Everything is fine.

But then why do I feel the urge to tell him the truth? Now that I think about it, my other friends bought my lame excuse "My family needed me. I don't wanna talk about it, sorry. But it's all good now" way too quickly. No questions asked. Why did they not care? Am I just a passing thought and they don't even wonder about me? Or am I just that good a liar?

I can tell him. I should tell him. Tim will understand. Tim can understand.

"My family needed me. I don't wanna talk about it, sorry. But it's all good now. You know how families can be."

He nods slowly, watching me intently. I'm uncomfortable under his gaze and I want to look away and fiddle with my hair, hide behind it. But I can't. It's a sign of a lie. I have to stay strong, fight the instinct for flight.

"Yeah, I know how they can be. So what happened?"

"I don't want to talk about it, ok?" I didn't mean to snap at him, but I'm so tense I think I'll rip apart any minute.

"I'm sorry, I didn't mean that."

"You kind of did. But it's ok. Shouldn't have pried."

"It's just … it ain't always easy to live with your own past, right? Sometimes it's really hard." Shit. I should not have said that. Shit, shit, shit. But I couldn't help myself. Even if I don't want to, with him things just slip out. I try to hold them in, but something about Tim is so enticing.

"Everyone has baggage. Cliché but true. But having someone to help you carry makes it feel less heavy."

"What's yours?"

"What's yours?"

"Secret for secret?" Tim leans back in his chair, before shooting forward, leaning across the table. Involuntarily I lean in as well until we are only inches apart.

"Why do you want to know?"

"A wise man once said that sharing baggage makes it lighter."

"Touché. Can I trust you?"

"If you didn't think you could, you wouldn't have let on that there is something to tell."

"Neither would you." We stare at each other, trying to read the other's mind. I have no idea what it could be. I don't think he struggles with the things I do. He is too collected for that. Then again, I can't be sure how I appear to others. Still, I doubt it. What could it be?

Do I really want to tell him mine though? Yes, I do. Can I? Yes, with him I can. I don't really have anything to base it on, yet I have this gut feeling that I can trust him completely and totally. But what if I am wrong? I'm not. I just am not.

Tim cracks his knuckles, making me wince.

"Don't." My hand shoots out before I can stop myself, covering his fingers. A slow smile spreads across his face, easing the tension that I wasn't even aware of until now.

"I can do much better." He challenges me with his gaze, teasing his fingers, willing them to crack.

"I'm serious, do not dare. I hate it." Too late.

"Kaya, over here!" Ruby is waving at me from across the crowded sushi bar. I haven't been here in so long that I take a few moments to savour the feeling of being back. The restaurant is modern and sleek, shiny surfaces all around. A staircase leads upstairs where the tables are because down on the ground level there is just a very long, windy sushi bar. The main part is taken up by the open kitchen, around which the bar snakes itself. Ruby, Hailey and Emily are already occupying our favourite corner. It's the perfect location to sit; you are at the edge so you can overlook the whole rest of the sushi bar, but it's also right at the corner of the kitchen, so we always just call out our orders to the chefs directly instead of waiting for our favourite rolls to pass us on the moving sushi belt.

"Hey, girls, sorry I'm late." I kiss each of them on the cheek, glad to be back.

"No worries, we saved you a seat." Ruby, with the typical determination with which she does absolutely everything in life, pulls me down on the bar stool next to her. I smile thanks and grab a plate of ginger off the rotating bar. Before saying anything else, I quickly devour it, enjoying its flavour. I love the unmistakable twinge that ginger has. It's difficult to describe, but I love it. The slightly bitter, yet fresh and almost sweet taste that I simply can't get enough of. Next to me, Ruby is doing the same. The other two hate it.

"So, Kaya, let's get straight down to it. Give us the lowdown on lunch." Hailey grins at me and sticks her tongue out.

"What are you after?" I try to feign innocence, not wanting to think about Tim that way. Not that there is any way to think about. We are friends, that's it.

Ruby's eyes are wide and curious. She loves gossip, seems to need it more than air sometimes.

"Oh come on, don't act coy. You're into him, it's so obvious."

"What?! Oh come on, Ruby, that's ridiculous. I barely know him."

"It's taken much less than that for you to fall for someone."

"Well, ya, maybe, but it's not like that. We genuinely are just friends. And we wanted to have lunch, just like friends do. We are all having dinner and there are no rumours about us double dating or something." She smacks my arm. Hard.

"Oh my god, you totally like him! How long has this been going on for?"

"I don't like him!"

"So you eat lunch with all your enemies?"

"I mean, I like him, but not like, like him." I look at my friends as if it's completely obvious. Guess for girls it kind of is. I see Emily wanting to say something, so I cut her off with waving gestures.

"But like, trust me, seriously, nothing. We are just friends, I mean I can do that right? No biggie. And he is really nice."

"He is. And you'll fall for him." I glare at Emily and she just grins back at me.

"It's true, sweetie. Face it."

"How about we'll just see?" Hailey is the only one who is being kind of rational. No way will I fall for Tim; there is no reason at all why I should.

"Fine, but be prepared to wait a really long time like, I don't know, forever."

"We'll see."

"Oh we will!"

"By the way have you guys seen the new episode of 'How I met your mother'?" And, just like that, the topic was dropped and we moved on. Guess that's something with friends; you can just change topic, spit-ball your thoughts and no one really cares. Everyone is the same that way. Things can change, thoughts can move on and so do conversations. It's easy, simple. Then why does it feel so false?

19

This is it. Here we go. 25 minutes and then it is over. Plus question time, but that'll be easy. You make up stuff, say some deep things and that's that. Here we go.

"Ok, guys, don't screw this up. I want this, badly. So I will personally strangle anyone who is in the way, get it?" That girl really needs therapy; she is way too intense. The little mouse next to me definitely agrees; her shoulders are basically up to her ears and she is clearly trying to hide. Poor Jessica, she does not seem to be able to take people well. Then again, I doubt anyone takes the red head well.

"We get it, you have serious controlling issues and are taking it out on us. Can we just go in there and get this over with? Then you can go back to ignoring us and we can all lead long, happy lives." Happy, ha, funny.

"Whatever." She stalks through the door and I mouth a silent "Thank you" at John, who winks at me.

"You ready for this?" He whispers it quietly as we walk into the classroom and take our places at the front.

"I sure hope so."

Our English teacher takes his seat; my cue to start.

"Welcome to our presentation on the book "Cut" by Patricia McCormick. We will be discussing …" I say my text, wait for the others to say theirs, jump in whenever

I have to and just keep praying that no one realizes that I'm shaking on the inside. I am terrified. My wrists are burning hot and I could swear that the metal on my bangles is melting away, exposing my skin and the scars forever engraved. I try to act nonchalant and am afraid it seems as false as it is. I pretend it's all ok; that everything's cool. I'm mortified to think what would happen if people realized how close this hits to home. I'm fine. No one realizes anything. It's all ok. It's all good.

"Thank you all so much for listening. We hope we didn't bore you too much." John's voice is drowned in the applause until the teacher gestures for everyone to calm down.

"Questions or topics for dicussion?" Angela is eager, and—I'm glad to see—obviously relieved. I'm assuming that means we did not screw up as badly as she expected us to.

Several people put up their hands. Breathe, Kaya, it's almost over.

"Uhm … Marc."

"I have a topic: Those people are totally just trying to kill themselves, it's sickening. Go ahead, everyone: discuss." What an idiot. He has no idea. I mean, yes, some of us. I mean, some of those kind of people. Not me, I'm over it. No more harming myself. I'm over it. I bore my nails into my hand, the pain sweet and welcome. It's hard to control my breathing, it's difficult not to scream. It's almost over, we can sit down soon. Just zoom out, Kaya.

Pretend you're listening, but don't. It's ok, no need to hear what these ignorant people have to say. It's all good.

I see people's lips move. I see their intense gesturing; their dedication to their own opinions. I can see it, but no sound is there. It's as if I'm deaf. The pulse of my own heart all I can hear. Is it baking hot in here?

I smile and nod, trying so hard to appear normal. It should be easy, I'm good at this. Then why does it feel so hard?

I catch John's eye and I smile. Relax my hands and my stance. Don't give anything away, Kaya. Keep it all in. Numb it out. My feelings, the voices, the gestures, the stares. Breathe, just breathe.

A foot nudges mine, I jump.

"Kaya. What is your opinion?" Our teacher is looking at me expectantly. John, standing next to me, gives me a prompting look. Angela is staring me down, willing me not to screw this up. As if this has anything to do with her grade. Jessica is glancing up at me through her lashes. And all other eyes in the room are on me.

It feels like the Californian sun has moved position and is shining down at me from the corner of the room—burning me up. My throat is parched, my hands are sweaty. My heart is racing and the blood is loud in my ears. Breathe, Kaya, breathe. I have to say something, anything.

"Uhm ... I think, it's quite controversial. There are a lot of viewpoints to be considered ..." Everyone is still staring. Not good enough, Kaya, not good enough. Story of my life. Not this time. I dig my nails into my palms, needing to feel something, anything.

"People often misunderstand it, I think. Just because someone self-harms does not mean they want to die. They just want to feel. If you wanted to die you'd have to cut lengthwise, but most don't. It's their own cry for help. Their own way of dealing with themselves and their lives. That's probably the worst. They know that things are maybe not as bad, rationally speaking, but they can't see that. They can't feel and it's all numb and isolated and alone. And it's all you have. All the pain that you can't feel, but you want it because at least it would tell that you are alive, even though you are dying on the inside. All of it is concentrated on that one spot and when you cut, you can release it. All the built up emotions and tensions just ooze out. And for just a moment, you're free. So I feel like people have distorted perceptions of self-harm and don't understand the reasoning behind it and therefore appoint it to a ridiculous stigma that simply isn't true."

There is silence. The teacher is nodding, scribbling something on his notepad. The pen, I hear it. It's that quiet. And it feels like ages, but it's only a split second. Then it starts. The whispers. The stares. The numbing pain spreading through my heart, pumped through my veins to the rest of my body. I can't think; it's all frozen. Lips are moving, people are talking. We are supposed to sit back down, another round of applause. Like a robot I move to my seat. I walk, I sit, I nod, I smile.

Everything is in a haze. I'm fighting the feelings of guilt that are trying to wash over me, swallow me, pull me down. Why did I just say all of that? I don't know, but it's not good. I can't deal, I just can't.

For once luck is on my side and this is my last period for the day. I can leave. The bell, that's all I need right now.

And as soon as it breaks through my self-imposed haze, I grab my things and shoot out of my chair, heading for the door before anyone else even has the chance to get up.

I wait in front of her office, nervously flicking through some magazines. I don't even know what I'm reading. Nor do I care, to be honest. What possibly could these magazines tell me that would contribute to my feeling better, safer?

The door opens and a woman in her mid 40s exits. Her eyes are a little red and she is clasping the sleeve of her shirt between her thumb and index finger. When her eyes sweep over me, she gives me a sad smile. There is so much pain within it, it's almost tangible. I smile back.

"It's going to be ok." My voice is soft and unexpected to both of us. She doesn't respond, but gives me another long look before disappearing through the door, out into the cruel world beyond these walls. She gets swallowed up and I just hope that I was right.

"Kaya? You ready?" I get up on shaky knees and mumble a greeting at Theresa as I take a seat on the couch. I feel exposed. This room, it strips you bare of your soul and thoughts. It drills down to the essence of your being.

Shifting uncomfortably, I finally slide down onto the floor, leaning against the couch, my arms propped on my knees. I make myself as small as possible, hoping I can hide and just disappear from the world. My therapist notes something down in her book.

"How are you today?" I notice I'm biting my lip when I feel the sharp taste of blood. Releasing my flesh from between my teeth, I think about her question. How am I? Scared, worried, anxious, numb.

But I don't say any of it. I keep it all bottled up inside. If I take the cap off, it could all spill. And then I'm empty and have nothing left inside.

Running my fingers through my hair, biting my thumb-nail. She's a therapist so she is probably reading tons into my actions. Isn't that basically their job? They analyse you, even if what you're doing is just a nervous habit. Then again, I guess that already gives away something about you.

"What happened to your hand?" I don't understand. I examine the back of my hand. It looks fine. Turning it around I spot the four marks in my palm. I curl my fingers inwards and it's obvious what caused them.

"Kaya, show me your wrists." I just shake my head, suddenly too tired to do anything. I just want to sleep. I'm so tired, so exhausted. I don't hear Theresa get up, but I feel her kneeling down beside me, taking my bangles off and examining the skin beneath them. It's standard, I've been through it a lot. Whenever I'm too numb or have hurt myself any other way, she has to check. Even if I refused, it's her therapeutic right.

She silently places the jewellery on the table in front of me. I feel her presence beside me; I know she hasn't left. She is waiting for something, I'm sure, but I just don't know for what.

"Kaya, tell me what happened." Her voice is soft, but insistent. I know that tone—that tone is not my friend. I just sit there, my eyes closed. I hate how exposed my wrists feel so I press them against my legs, hiding them from Theresa and the world. I really want to put on my bracelets, to feel their weight and security. But I'm not going to give Theresa the satisfaction. To be fair, she probably wouldn't see it as winning, but I'd feel like I'm losing.

"Kaya, please. Anything, what is on your mind?" I'm tired. Tired of silence, tired of words, tired of this, tired of that.

"You know how they say that when you get knocked down, you're supposed to get back up?" I wait for her to say something, but she doesn't. I'm assuming she nodded, but it's not enough. I'm waiting, still quiet. I need her reassurance, I need to hear something. I wait.

"That's the saying, yes." Thank you.

"I think that might be true, but with every fall, getting up is harder. And eventually it's easier just not to. Well, it's always easier not to, but at some point you lose the reason why you should."

"And you feel you've reached that point?" In the darkness behind my lids I can see the students in my class, their whispers and stares. I see the white hospital room, and my mom and dad. I see nights when I just felt like I was losing it, all alone in my room and my mind. I see the tissues soaked with blood on the bathroom floor. But I also see Tim's face; his smile, his text. I see Hailey when we were at MAC a while ago.

"I don't think you ever know."

20

So were you serious?

About?

What you said at lunch …

Tim, you've got to give me more info than that.

Secret for secret.

I guess … I don't know. U?

I don't know. I mean, if you don't want to, then …

You want to, don't you? Why?

I never said that.

Reading between the lines. Look, I'd like to know your story. I wanna help if I can.

It's in the past.

I meant be there for you – shared baggage is lighter, right?

Right. So secret for secret?

Ya. So when do you wanna do this 'reveal'?

Idk …

Neither do I.

Guess whenever the time is right …

Ya, sure. Go with the flow and all.

Totally. G2g, ttyl :* <3

Ttyl :* <3

21

It's worse than before. The voices, the looks, the people. It's as if there is this glass wall between them and me; I can hear and see everything and sadly so can they, but I can't reach them. But they can reach me—guess that kind of destroys my glass wall metaphor. This time around they are not being subtle at all; open whispers, open stares. Never into my eyes though. Just at my skin, my wrists. I feel their eyes travelling over me, wondering what is beneath my clothing. And, of course, today of all days I chose to wear a thin long sleeved shirt. Not necessarily because I'm cold—it's San Diego, that isn't really an option—but because of comfort. Being able to pull the sleeves down to my fingers, clasping the fabric like my life depends on it—it's soothing, something to do. Except now I can't. I've rolled up my sleeves, giving people full view of my arms. I have nothing to hide—that's what it's supposed to say. I doubt anyone is listening to my message.

I can feel people's eyes on me when I turn my back. All day I wish that I am invisible. It's scary, it's annoying. Am I paranoid? I turn around, hoping to catch people. And I always do. I doubt that the whole school is talking, but it feels like it. It feels like I'm surrounded by this crowd and I am the only topic of interest. The need to hide my arms is overwhelming, but I fight it. I try to swallow the anxiety within me. I try to drown it out, to put on the same smile I've been using for years. But I can't. Suddenly I'm tired, exhausted, drained. And yet I have to put on the performance of my life.

Every new class is torture. That's the thing about teenager—we talk. We gossip. All I can hope for is that by tomorrow, or even earlier, something else will have happened. It will blow over, maybe be at the back of people's minds. But soon it'll move further and further back until it disappears completely, until it's only a memory for me. Until just another empty, hollow spot within me is the only reminder of this day, this hour, this minute and agony. For years and months all I wanted was to feel. Now I do. And I wish I could take it back. But I don't want to be numb either. I can't do that again. It always feels like I'm just a step away from the cliff. If I fall, eventually I won't be able to get back up. If I break, no one will be able to fix me.

There are people from my English Literature class in latterly each of my other classes. So whenever I walk in, I see their eyes on me. Sometimes a flicker crosses their face; just a moment, but a moment is enough to change it all. It only took me a moment to end everything. It only takes them a moment to remember and to tell someone else. And then a moment for them to turn their heads as well; a day full of moments of pain, a day filled with moments that push me away from myself just that much more every time.

I'm afraid of Biology. This is it. He will have heard, I'm sure. As I walk into the classroom, I'm reminded of the day we met. How we were strangers sharing our lives. Now soon we will be strangers sharing a past. Facing my other friends, that felt easier. They acted like it was alright. Maybe after years of knowing each other forgiveness is easier. Maybe some even feel guilty. And maybe some just think it's rumors. It doesn't matter to me. It never will. Tim, on the other hand, does. I can't explain, but I want his approval.

The few steps to our desk seem like a long march. It seems like it will never end, stretching out endlessly, a path of insecurity and scrutiny. He must hear or sense me coming because he lifts his head. Our eyes meet. He smiles.

It's dark. In my room, outside and in my heart. I check my clock. 11:37pm. Still hours to go until sunrise. I turn on my bedside lamp and grab my book. Sense of an ending. It's a good story, interestingly narrated and compelling. But tonight I can't get into it. I read the same page many times and yet I don't know what it's about. My heart feels constricted; my stomach clenches and my throat is dry. I'm breathing deeply, I can't help myself. Throwing my book to the floor, I bury my face in my cushion. I feel as if I am suffocating, but it's only wishful thinking. I clench my fists, boxing into my pillow over and over again until I exhaust myself. I bite my lip, press my hands onto my closed eyelids as if trying to shut out the world.

I can't breathe, I can't feel. Numbness overcomes me. I slide off my bed onto my knees. I'm cold, freezing. My feet are icicles. I lay my head on the bed, crying without tears. I whimper, sound catching in my throat. It can't escape; the world will never hear it.

I feel hollow, alone and so empty. It's as if I am dying inside. As if my heart was slowly becoming ashes, blowing away in the hollowness of myself. I feel numb. Sad, lonely and yet it's more in my heart than any feeling. I don't have any energy to scream, to cry. I just want to feel. I hate this. I hate being caught in myself. Having wings and not being able to fly—this is how it must feel. Tied down, restricted, broken.

I feel alone here. I don't want to die. I just want the peace. I just want to recognize myself. I get up with lots of difficulties. My knees are shaking as I slowly walk to my full length mirror. I stare. I see an ugly, fat girl looking back at me. Her chubby legs are pale and look terrible in her soft sleep shorts. Her stomach is 3D, fat and bulging. Her chin is too wide and fat, ugly. There is no other word. Her face is too round, her hair too frizzy. Her legs are too short. And her eyes. They are sad, lonely, empty. In the dim light they appear black. Her makeup is poorly removed and her eyes are brimming with unshed tears. She scrunches her face, willing them to spill over. Any sign of emotion. I'm tired of feeling so numb.

One tear makes it down her cheek. It looks as lost as she does. Alone in a world of darkness.

Abruptly I turn away. I can't do this anymore. I need to feel, I need to know I am alive. I've died inside too many times to just breathe in. I need to free myself. I need relief.

Walking to my drawer I slide my hand underneath my old stuffed animals. They have been sitting in there for years. Memories of happy, soft times. I pull out the Swiss Army Knife. It's heavy in my hand. It feels warm, welcome.

I sit down, my legs propped up. My wrist is bare, exposed. It's hard to see in this light, but I know they are there: the scars, the memories. How no one ever noticed them is a mystery to me. Then again, people can be as ignorant as they want. They may see them but shut it out. Blame it on the light, on my bracelets, on an optical illusion. Or maybe their brains register it; selfpreservation mode. People are so selfish. I'm one of the worst. I keep hurting others. Worrying others, annoying others—making everyone's life unnecessarily hard. No wonder they ignore the scars. People like to believe the lies "I am fine". They don't want the truth; they don't want to see the pain. And that's all these scars are—a manifestation of the pain inside. The pain and the numbness. You'd think they couldn't co-exist, but somehow they do. They both consume me completely. On the one hand, I am in agony, hurting so badly. On the other, I don't feel a thing. I know I should, but I can't. Guess that's what the pain is—the pain of not feeling, the pain of facing nothingness. Maybe the pain is like when you miss someone—not having them at your side hurts. Not feeling anything—that hurts too. So I try to make myself feel. To know I am alive. I cut my wrists because I need it. It's pretty stupid in a way; wrists are harder to hide. And yet maybe that is why; maybe I want people to see, to know. Just to ask me "Are you alright?" Just to know someone cares. But no one does. No one wants to see. I lightly trace the scars with the blade. I'm calmer already. Now I am in control. It's up to me, I can make myself feel again.

Knowing it would be stupid to break through the skin on my wrists that my counsellor and parents check religiously, I stretch out my legs and pull my shorts down a little. Just enough to expose my hips. My insides clench and I double over, breathing hard. With my index finger I stroke my pale skin. I position the blade.

As much as I wish I had a choice, I know I don't. It's one of those moments when although you need to contemplate something, ultimately you know what you're going to choose. I always know what I choose.

A tingle runs through my whole body. It feels like all my nerves are on alert; they know this. They expect it, know what's coming, anticipate it. Numb pain fills my heart and

I want to scream. But I can't. So for the first time in months I give in. I let myself fall, I let myself feel.

I cut.

22

"Kaya, you look terrible. I mean, gorgeous, but really tired. Are you ok?" Her pitch of voice hurts my ears. It's dripping sweet, sticky so.

"Slept badly." She regards me with a look, curious and cautious. But most of all greedy. She wants something and I doubt I want to give it to her. In fact, I know I don't. Because whatever I say, she'll interpret it the way she wants. She'll take whatever she wishes. Or she won't even listen. She won't even care. Ruby has never been very open-minded. I know her stance towards drugs, smoking, tattoos and pretty much anything else that isn't perfectly preppy. I can pretty accurately guess what she thinks of this.

"You poor thing. Too much on your mind?" Reaching out, she pats my arm. Her eyes are big, puppy-dog like. I've observed the look many times. She uses it to appear trustworthy and sincere. I know better.

"Nah, just one of those nights." She isn't satisfied, it's obvious. Yet she tries to hide it, like she always does. Masquerade—her favourite movie. Wonder why.

"Well, if you want to talk about it, I'm always here for you, ok?"

"What about during all those months in Switzerland? Your letters must have gotten lost." Her smile stays, her gaze sways to angry and upset, before settling back on concerned.

"Babe, I wanted to give you time with your family. And I did call, though time difference was obviously an issue. Nine hours is a lot." There is no point.

"Ya, sorry. Restless night equals cranky me. No harm done?"

"Never. But ya, I'm here for you, always."

"Thanks, Ruby. I know that."

"Catch you later, bye honey." She blows me a kiss, disappearing out the door. I lean over the sink, trying not to be sick. Replaying the exchange in my head I'm trying to figure out what details she'll spin out of proportion. I can't know, it could be anything. She is good at what she does.

I see her walking towards me. She was ill yesterday so she missed that whole episode. But now she is coming. I have been dodging her all day, coming to class just on time, but too late for any conversation. And then at the end of class I shot out of my seat, mumbling an excuse about having to see my guidance counsellor and practically ran out of the room. But now here comes the moment.

Hailey smiles at me. She opens her arms and I step into them; reluctantly, but glad. She smells like Hailey. I close my eyes for a moment, breathing her in. My best friend pulls back, placing her hands on my hips. I suppress a wince as she touches the tender spot.

"How are you?" Her voice is low, relaxed and yet insistent. She is watching carefully, and it takes a lot of strength not to avoid her gaze.

"I'm good. Tired, but good. How about you? Feeling better?" She doesn't skip a beat.

"Ya, much. So how are things with Tim?" A wicked gleam sneaks into her eyes and she raises her eyebrows. I smack her and pretend to pout.

"Stop it! You know there is nothing going on?"

"I'm sure."

"Good."

"I know." The knot in my stomach has disappeared. This is Hailey, this is us. The smiles, the teasing, the hugs, the closeness. Even though she does not know this, she's always been able to break through my wall. When everyone else's touch makes me feel captured, hers gives me wings. My love for this girl flows so deep, I can't even fathom it.

I really did miss her. That's the good thing about friends, true ones, at least. Even if you can't see them and even if you don't miss them, they are still there. It wasn't that I didn't miss Hailey; it was rather that I couldn't feel. Missing someone just wasn't in my vocabulary.

"Kaya." Even if I hadn't recognized the voice, I'd know from Hailey's slow, righteous smile who is calling.

"Don't", I whisper, before turning to face Tim.

"Hey, Hailey."

"Hey, Tim. I'll leave you two. Catch you later, babes."

She gives me a quick peck on the cheek, sneakily breathing into my ear.

"Go get the hottie." She ducks away before my hand connects with her and I hear Tim laugh.

"Do I even want to know?"

"Probably not." We smile at each other. Even though it's only a moment, it feels like ages. His blue eyes are as clear as the sky today and they are twinkling. I could get lost in them; completely and utterly forgetting time. Just those beautiful eyes and me, for now and ever.

"You do that a lot." His voice is low and I have to strain to hear him over the end-of-the-day noise in the hallway.

"Do what?" His index finger touches his lips and my eyes are drawn to them.

"Bite your lip." I try to hide the surprise from my face. I know I do, but I just didn't think he'd notice. Or I never even gave it any thought.

"I'm pretty observant."

"Clearly."

"You ready to go?"

"Almost." I dial the combination for my locker, pulling it open. A wave of my own perfume greets me, enveloping me like a familiar hug. I grab the books I need, carelessly stuffing them into my bag. Tim watches me with amusement, clearly pleased though that I followed his advice and always carry a bag with me now.

"Let's go."

"Thank you." I take my Chocolate Frappucino off the counter and walk towards the table for two at the back of the coffee shop, where Tim is already seated, calmly sipping his own drink. He smiles at me when I take a seat, pushing his cup away a little. For a moment he just looks at me. I feel scrutinized under his gaze and I have to look away, letting my eyes stray.

"So, I've been thinking … I definitely want to know what Hailey said." I feel my cheeks turning crimson.

"Uhm, I don't know what you're talking about", I claim, trying to avoid his eyes. Too bad he is not fooled so easily.

"Oh come on. Before in school? What did she say? You can tell me anything. Please." He looks at me, his eyes smoldering. In this light his eyes are almost grey and intense. Not for the first time do I feel stripped off all my lies and acting. I wonder how deep into my soul he can see; how many layers of blackness he has already come across. His eyes beg with me and it takes all my strength not to give in.

"Ya, sure. I could tell you I am terrorist and about to blow up this Starbucks and you wouldn't mind."

"Well, I'd mind, but you could still tell me. We'll have our reveal eventually, remember? That kind of demon-strates that we can tell each other anything."

"True. But I just may not want to", I say slowly. Then I hesitate; do I really not want to tell him everything? I was tempted once before, why not give in? I stare out the window. I think he is saying something, but I am not listening. I'm caught in my thoughts, in my world. Tell him. Reveal it. And then whether or not he wants to run is his choice.

He seems to have noticed the change in my expression because his words just kind of let off and he just watches me intently. I sit back, surprised at how close we are leaned in.

"You ok?" Nodding slowly, I contemplate the question. Am I ok?

"Do you want to go for a walk? It's too loud in here." I hope he'll say yes, but I am afraid of if he does. He looks at me for a moment longer, as if he is searching for something in my face. Whatever he found must have convinced him because, finally, he nods.

We're walking through the streets, both of us silent. Me, wondering how to start and what it actually is that I have to say. Him, sensing—as so often—exactly what I want; he appears to have such a good feeling for what someone needs and what they don't. It has surprised me already a couple of times; he noticed that I don't like people touching me and he somehow also knows when to leave me alone and when I'm in the mood to be social. Sometimes, to be honest, I've asked myself if he can read my mind.

I sigh and look up at Tim with his gorgeous features which, even though I've only known him a short time, already seem so familiar. I'm now determined where I want to go, and what I want to tell him. I lead the way into the park around the corner and sit down on my favorite bench away from everyone else. Even though I sense his presence next to me, I can't make myself look at him. Not yet.

I'm staring at a patch of grass in front of me. It's muddy, not fresh and green anymore. It looks destroyed; too many people have trampled on it carelessly. And the more spoiled it became, the more people should have thought about it. But in the end, a simple "Well, if it's only me" convinced them to step on the same spot nevertheless. And the patch of grass lost its radiance. It became muddy and used.

I take a deep breath, hold it, let it out. This is it. I look up to meet his expectant gaze.

"Reveal, right?" He nods slowly, clearly trying to figure out where this is going.

"You can still back out. No hard feelings."

"Anything, Kaya. Anything." This time it's me who is nodding. I squeeze my eyes shut. This is the first time I've ever told anyone. My relatives know, but it was never me who told them. And even though my therapists always wanted to hear my account of things, really, they already knew it all. This here is my choice; this is all me.

With a sigh I open my eyes and slide all my bracelets off my wrist into my lap. I can't look at him; not now. I am afraid, clutching my wrist with my hand.

"Here goes" I whisper, not sure who I am trying to warn. Slowly I stretch out my arm, palm facing upward. I hear him almost inaudibly suck in his breath.

Although people somewhere in the park are talking and I can hear kids' voices and cars, although I know that life is continuing all around us, it feels as if it is all standing still. I hear everything dampened. I am underwater, looking up. The life above me is reflected in the water, but even though I can see it, I am not part of it. The only thing I hear is the rush of the water, my heartbeat. And now, shakily and quiet yet so penetrating, my own voice.

"On February 19th I tried to kill myself."

23

There. I said it. This is it. It's out. No more taking it back; the evidence is too obvious. Cards on the table. I don't wait for his response; I can't. I need to let it out, the words are filling my mouth and I need to get rid of them before they suffocate me.

"A treatment facility and home, here in San Diego, that's where I've been staying these past few months. I took antidepressants, but they didn't only dim the bad feelings, the pain inside, but also the good stuff. Though there wasn't a lot of it. It was all dark, sometimes still is. Darkness has been surrounding me for so long, I can't even pinpoint when it started. Minutes of sadness and feeling down turned into hours which turned into days and eventually into weeks. Weeks with barely a smile, no laughter. None of it real at least. I did laugh, I did smile, but inside I was crying; inside I was dying. My feelings would just get so built up I couldn't handle it. I used to go for runs but I was often too tired and weak." I laugh drily.

"Barely eating anything can do that to a person. So I needed something else. At that point it wasn't just feeling sad, I guess I could kind of deal with that. It was more than that; it was not feeling. People say they get what I mean, you know the doctors and all, but really they don't. It's like an anesthesia for your heart, you know. I was numb. Dying inside. And then one day I just … cut. More like a scratch, actually, but it felt amazing. The high was incredible. The feeling of feeling. Then it became deeper. That trickle of blood was so soothing. Pain I could control. Something I was in charge of. I meant for it to be only that one time or so, but it wasn't. The next time I felt close to exploding, I did it again. I didn't even think about it, I swear it just happened. The first few months it was never very deep and not often, but the way my skin burned felt so incredibly good. I told myself that it was nothing, that I wasn't doing it deeply so it was not something serious. I truly believed that I could stop whenever I wanted. But I never did. I never wanted to. But I was sure I could and that's the difference between an addict and someone who just does something: one can stop, the other can't. And then everything got worse. Grades, friends, home. A "vicious cycle of deep-rooted issues". I've heard the terms way too often. You know, it's hard to answer the question "What's wrong?" when nothing's right. And nothing was right. Nothing I did was good enough, ever. My grades were slipping and my parents were complaining, but if occasionally I did bring home an A, they didn't care. My dad was always so good in school and he used to be so proud of me being the same way that it got to him. And my mum; so often do I hear how beautiful she is and I agree, but it's just hard not to feel like you're competing with that. Not to feel like you'll never be the same way. So I tried to lose weight. Purging after meals, eating very little, that kind of stuff. When my mum found out, hell broke loose. Never would she have wanted a daughter with an eating disorder. She kept complaining how thin I was, when before I felt too fat. When before she even said I was too fat. Not in as many words, but I'm paraphrasing. I never managed to just be ok, to have them accept me. And it sucks, believe me. Not feeling like even your family accepts you. On good days I now see that I was wrong. But it's hard. And then I couldn't take it anymore. I don't know what it was that day, probably something simple, some misunderstanding. Maybe a wrong look, a word that didn't fit for me … I don't remember. But it was enough to send me over the edge. I tried to escape. I didn't want to kill myself, and yet I did. It doesn't make sense, but I knew it would be the end; I hoped it would be. But I just couldn't think about that. I wasn't thinking, I wasn't feeling. I needed something; I needed that. I took the knife, and then I woke up hours later in the hospital. You have no idea how disappointed I was. To be there, to be breathing, to be alive, when I felt so dead inside. But, I don't know why, though these past months have been so terrible, I didn't do it again. I know I could have, but somehow the knowledge of that made me go on. I always tell myself " One more day. If nothing changes, then you can do it." And somehow that helps. I still feel the pain inside, I still often feel hollow and worthless and all alone in the world, but somehow I also feel alive. I feel, something I haven't done in a while. But every time darkness washes over me, I'm afraid that I'll slip away from myself all too soon." I shut my mouth, sure to have scared him off. I close my eyes for a moment, memories overcoming me. My first appointment with Theresa, the nights I woke up screaming or wouldn't go to sleep in the first place, the days at the hospital. And again and again that moment in which it all changed. That moment when all the relief and pain of the world joined together; when I cut myself too deeply intending that to be the last thing I'd ever do.

"Why don't you like to be touched?" The quiet question breaks the silence and lingers there for a moment. It's not what I expected and I look at him in astonishment and gratefulness. I meet his eyes and get lost in them for a second before I can answer. The understanding in them seems endless. Even though I try, I can't find the judgment or disgust that I feared. Just a friend looking back at me.

"I don't know." It's true. I don't. Tim doesn't say anything, just sits there.

"I mean, I never used to have a problem with it. Hugs from my friends, even if they had no idea how I felt, were always comforting and reassuring. But after I woke up, they suddenly felt restricting. Like something bad. An attempt to keep me here, to not let me get away. Gosh, this sounds crazy." I bury my face in my hands.

"No. It doesn't, and it's not." I feel him watching me as we sit in silence for a while.

"Kaya …" I sense his reluctance. My body goes rigid. I feel vulnerable and exposed; naked without my jewelry. I put my bracelets back on, not daring to break the silence. He will have to continue.

Tim gets up and my heart sinks. He is running. He is leaving. This is it.

"I have to process this. Give me time, please." He touches my shoulder briefly before walking away. I watch him, his figure disappearing in the greenery of our surroundings until I had stared at the distance so long that I don't even remember at which point I lost him.

I don't remember exactly how I got home. I can guess, but I don't know. It's all a haze. I keep checking my phone. I want him to write me. I want his message. I need it; I need him.

"Honey, you're home."

"Obviously." My mother smiles at me affectionately.

"How was your day?"

"It was ok. Nothing too special." Lie. "I'm gonna go upstairs, I have work."

"Ok, I'll call you for dinner."

The stairs seem endless and when I get upstairs, I just throw myself on my bed. But I'm exhausted, so it's more of a violent lying down than actually flinging myself. I can't even get that right.

Sometimes it's hard to figure out when it all went wrong. Actually, it's always hard. It's something that has been haunting me for a long, long time. I hope that if I can pinpoint the moment it all went wrong, I could just make it right. Preferably reverse it all, but even in my most despairing moments I never believed that that would be a possibility. But to just set it right. To prevent further pain inflicted to myself or the ones I love.

I know I'm cold to my parents, especially my mom. But it's not because of what she does, or at least not only. It's because of how I feel. So guilty for all that's happened. So if I could just find the moment that triggered it all. Maybe then I'd be able to forgive myself, everyone else and the world.

But instead of getting closer to figuring out when it all started, I feel like I'm drifting further away from that moment. I keep messing up, I keep being depressed and alone and in darkness, when really I should be much better by now. I want to walk towards the light, but it feels as if it's being dimmed. I have good moments, I used to have good weeks even after I got out of treatment. Those were amazing. So surreal to feel normal and to laugh and to smile and to just be upset at times. I've been through a lot, that's ok. It was hard to let myself feel. Too hard. I can't even figure it out the second time around; when did everything go bad since February? I just don't know. I never seem to.

My phone vibrates in my pocket and makes me jump.

"God", I murmur, contemplating if I should check

the message or leave it until later. I hate it when people don't answer immediately; it drives me crazy. I can't impose that on others. I pull my cell out of my pocket and my heart stops.

Whatsapp Message: Tim Weaver

My heart picks its beat back up, but at a quicker pace. My phone nearly slips out of my hand, it's that sweaty. Before reading the message, I close my eyes and think about Tim. His blue eyes, blond hair. His strong hands, his slightly crooked smile. The way his white teeth are the best sign that I was able to make him smile or laugh. His soothing presence, the way he may not say that much but observes everyone. He must pick up on so much, see people so much more clearly than most of us. If I had known him, say two years ago, would he have saved me from myself? Had we passed on a random street on a random day, would he have been able to read my story in my eyes?

Do you regret telling me?

The question catches me off guard. I didn't expect it, of all things he could have so easily said. Do I regret it? No.

No.

I can tell he is online so he must be thinking about my response. I hate it when people do this; typing, online, typing, online, typing … I always wonder what they are think-ing, doing. What they decide not to write, not to send.

Ok. Tim, one of the really observant people I know … he must have noticed. I need to know.

Did you know?
Know what?
My story. Or parts of it; any of it.

I realize that I am biting my lip, so I let it go and attack my thumbnail instead. The suspense is killing me; I hate waiting, never have been very patient, much less so since everything I've been through.

Rumours. That you cut yourself.
Did you believe them?
I don't know. A bit; you are so protective of your wrists. I've noticed in class and stuff. And someti-mes your whole body goes rigid and you scratch your wrists and then start fidgeting.

I'm absolutely stunned. I never realized any of this. Not that I was doing it, nor that he saw. I can't take this. I just can't.

G2g, byebye :*
Ok. Bye :* <3

I stare at the heart for a moment, cherishing the fact that he sent me one. Cherishing the friend I got to keep.

24

I'm nervous and excited and looking forward to seeing Tim from the moment I woke up. Nervous, because I can't quite judge how he'll react. I think I can be pretty sure that I get to keep my friend; but that does not guarantee any certain reaction of any kind. Then again, he did kind of believe some of the rumors. They touched on some parts of it, so I suppose if he was relaxed about it before, then maybe he still is. But what if he is not? That's the little voice inside of me. The evil, mean voice. The one that scares me. It tells me the truth about how I really look and am. I guess that could mean it is right this time around as well. But hope dies last—maybe I still have a chance.

"Kaya!" I startle, mumbling an automatic "sorry" as my mom and dad eye me wearily across the table.

"Where are your thoughts lately? Anything concerning you?" My mom's fearful gaze makes me roll my eyes. Too late I remember how much she hates it. I see her throw my dad a look.

"Darling, we need to talk."

"Now? I kinda have to go to school in a bit."

"This won't take long. It's not really a talk. You just have to listen." Although my dad says this with a smile, my insides clench. This can't be good. It never is. I nod

cautiously, watching my parents. I guess it's a kid thing—
you learn to read the signs, the intonations in your parents' voices, the little changes in their eyes. Anything that
could indicate that you are in trouble: a survival instinct
of modern children.

"Honey you know we love you. I mean, we really
do. And …" My mom looks at my dad helplessly,
struggling for words.

"What your mother is trying to say is that yes, we
love you. And we have your best interests at heart. You
are our everything. This family has been through some
things in the past few months, and we know that you
probably think we've been overly cautious and lenient,
and maybe we have let it carry on too long. But we want
you to be safe and happy, and have a future ahead of you.
We don't want any doors closing for you. Which is why
we are concerned about your school work."

He just lets that sit there. They look at me as if I am
supposed to confirm or deny their concerns. Denial
would probably be the most teenaged thing to do, but I
can't. My mind is having troubles keeping up from Tim
to the talk to schoolwork. It's only 7:30 a.m. after all.

When it's almost awkwardly clear that they are not
going to get an answer, my dad continues.

"You don't seem to be studying a lot lately or spending much time doing homework or revising. We just
don't think you can afford not to work after such a long
absence."

I burst.

"Not to work? I work! Efficiently and at lunch and after school and in the evenings … just because you don't see me do it, does not mean I don't."

"Sweetie, that's not what we are implying … "

"Ya, you're not implying it, you're saying it. And it's not true."

"You do have a history of letting your work slip and trying to cover it up, leaving things to the last minute."

"That was last year."

"Well you haven't really proven otherwise. We're sorry, Kaya, but this is what we are seeing. And by previous experience …"

"Previous experience? You mean the time right before I tried to kill myself?"

The impact of my words lingers in the room. They look at me, stunned. We never talk about it in such angry terms. We never really talk about it at all. Sure, it's referred to, but that's it. My voice is more bitter than I intend it to be, but I can't help it:

"For months you treat me like I am going to break at any moment and now suddenly this attack on my work ethic? Which, by the way, you have no idea about. I'm going to be late for school."

I storm out of the kitchen, wishing desperately that I could storm out of the house and find my own way to school. But, unfortunately, I'm stuck with my mom driving me. I walk to the car, get in, slam the door and plug in my earphones. I need something loud, something angry. Scrolling through my playlist I crank Pink up loud, not caring if I'm being rude. I'm not the one who should be apologizing.

Only as we are turning the corner in front of my High School and I see all the other teenagers spilling into the main building do I remember Tim. Great! Of course they had to go and ruin my buzz on the one morning I was actually kind of excited to get up on. Well it's too late now. It always is.

"Oh my gosh, oh my gosh, oh my gosh! Kaya!" I turn around just in time to catch my balance when Hailey flings her arms around me. I wince partly at the impact, partly at the proximity. She pulls back, shaking me. The world goes dizzy and I wrench free.

"What the hell? Stop it!" I really don't have the energy for her energy. I'm still annoyed at my parents, and I really don't need Hailey invading my privacy as well. She seems completely unaffected by my anger though, grinning from ear to ear. Now she starts jumping up and down, clapping her hands like a giddy toddler. This day just keeps getting better.

"If anyone here has the right to be angry, that'd be me— the ignored, oblivious best friend. But I'm too excited to care! Although I'll probably bring it up again whenever I need a favour."

"What are you talking about? And stop jumping, seriously." She rolls her eyes, but follows my command. I look around, uncomfortable. Some people are staring at us. To be fair, I would too, if I could. But I hate being stared at. To escape the snickers and curious looks, I take her hand and pull her across the hall into the girls' bathroom. Maybe I'll drown her in a toilet or something as long as it makes her shut up and leave me alone.

A senior girl with long black hair is standing at the mirror, combing it. She gives us a bored look and continues.

"So what's up?"

"What's up?!" Hailey's voice is high pitched and too loud, echoing off the walls. The senior girl looks at us annoyed, though clearly doing her best to ignore us. I wish I could, too.

I feel like I'm in some movie, missing something crucial. Because whatever Hailey is so excited about, it must be big. She doesn't get that excited over small things—she always has her priorities in order.

She is my best friend, I know that. But although I am sure it's some big news, I doubt it is life changing. Or at least not mine. And I have other things to deal with right now. My parents, for example. My bipolar, schizophrenic, annoying, patronizing parents. Or Tim and what he thinks of me. How is he going to act, what is going to happen next? Or a million other things that I'm sure I could come up with would I not be stuck in the bathroom with my best friend whose smile could quite literallly reach the moon right now.

"How can you be so calm? I'm freaking out and it's not even me who it's happening to!"

"Well, it's clearly not me either because I have no idea what you are talking about." I hiss my words, unable to keep my irritation in any longer. Suddenly her smile fades. The excitement in her eyes is overshadowed by hurt. Instinctively I bite my lip; I hate putting that look on her face, even when I don't know why what I said was wrong and provoked this reaction.

"You're seriously not going to tell me? I thought we were closer than that." Gosh, will you get on with it? It takes a lot of willpower not to roll my eyes. I've never been a patient person, but my temper has gotten much worse since all that happened. Irritability—one of the negative aspects of not taking my meds. True, I have ways to deal with it but right now I don't have time for it. Or the energy or the positive attitude.

"Hailey, I don't have time for this. What is it?" I know I sound impatient, but I can't help it. There is only so much I can take, and I don't need many little things pushing me towards a breaking point. I hate secrets. Though I guess that makes me quite the hypocrite. Well, I've never claimed to be a saint and we all have our flaws. Me more than others.

"You know what, forget it. I was happy for you, but you clearly don't wanna share."

"For God's sake, share what?" She stares at me, disbelief on her face. I stare back, irritation dominating my features, no doubt there.

"The fact that you and Tim had a date." Her voice is cold, but it slips a little. I know she is hurt. But I have no idea what the hell she is talking about. This must be some stupid joke. Maybe he put everyone up to it. I would never have suspected that. Never suspected him to be this cruel—to rub it in that, apparently, it was all an act and I had lost him as a friend. What else could this be? It's not like she could be serious.

"What the hell? You know that's so not true. And if it were, obviously I'd tell you."

"Like you told Ruby?" That explains. Ruby always explains everything.

"I didn't tell Ruby anything because it's not true. Ya, Tim and I had coffee, but not a date. Seriously, Hailey, I can't deal with this right now. Please, you know Ruby, causing trouble and all."

"It's a little too late to talk your way out of this. You just basically admitted it."

"Hailey, stop." I can't do this. Not now, not ever. Not with her.

"I just cannot believe it. It's like I don't even know you anymore."

"I'm serious, shut up. I mean it." I turn towards the sink, splashing cold water on my face. I can't deal.

"No, I mean it. Talk to me when the Kaya I know is back." She turns around to leave. I try to hold it in, try to swallow it. It's hard, the words want to escape my mouth. All the whispers and stares and pretense. I can't anymore. I can't make more cracks in my life; I've already made too many. But the words are bubbling inside of me; the anger pulsing through my veins. I hear my blood rushing.

"The Kaya you know? Hailey you have no idea! You haven't for ages now. If you really knew me, you wouldn't believe me like every other idiot around here does. And you're blaming me! Ruby is a bitch, we both know it!" I scream the words that I've held in for way too long. I can't cope with their weight, can't deal with them gnawing at me. The shock on her face should stop me, but it doesn't. It's too late, the avalanche has been shot loose, and the rest is just collateral damage. That's what it all boils down to, isn't it? Collateral damage. On the path of destroying myself I've taken too many people down with me. And I hate it, I hate myself for it. But really, it doesn't stop me. It never did, never would. It might slow down my spiral for a bit but in the end it doesn't change a thing. None of them do. Collateral damage that is irrevocable when you die inside; the collateral damage necessary to free me of my life.

"You chose to just believe all the lies. You're my best friend, shouldn't you know me better? Shouldn't you insist? Come on, it's the elephant in the room. You have to have heard the stupid rumours. The ridiculousness of it all. And you have to know how much of it hits home. Or are you really that ignorant? Guess I got you all wrong, too. And I thought we were closer than that." I spit those last words in her face; words I've been holding in for too long. Congratulations, Theresa, you achieved your goal of teaching me about honest communication.

I run. I hear her high pitched scream, but I drown out the words and bolt out the door. I need to get out of here. I can't be here. I just can't.

I rush to the office, to the nurse's room. Knocking on the door, I shiver. My body convulses in waves as the words all come back to me. The look on her face, the sting of my words. I hate what I did to her. I hate what it did to me.

"Sweetheart, are you ok? What's wrong? Come on, lie down." The nurse, Kate, as I can read on her name tag, takes me by the hand and leads me to the bed. I'm sobbing loudly, empty. No tears are coming. I've trained myself to hold those back until I am all alone and no one can see or hear.

"Tell me what's wrong? Are you hurt?" Her concern touches me. She worries for me and she has no idea what a terrible person I am. She does not know that I just drove a knife through my best friend's heart. She probably doesn't even suspect how I made my parents age by many years, and how I make every day for them hell by just being. They think it's good that I'm alive—but they are wrong. Yes, it would have hurt them had I died the day I was supposed to. But they'd move on eventually. Now they live in constant fear—constant worry. That's not a life I want for them. It's collateral damage—but it doesn't mean it doesn't hurt me with every breath, every look I give them. Every movement when they don't feel like I'm watching them. The anxiety in their hands, the pain in their eyes.

And Kate is asking me if I am hurt. I want to laugh, it strikes me as that funny. But I can't. I can't laugh anymore. I can't pretend.

"Nauseous", I manage to breath.

"I see. Did you throw up?" I nod, hoping it'll make her excuse me for the rest of the day. And then it's weekend and I can just hide in my bed; no need to think, talk, eat, smile.

"Ok, Sweetie. Do you want me to call your parents to come pick you up?" I nod feebly, too exhausted to speak. She pats my head and I want to scream. My heart is tied with anxiety, and I feel like I'm going to explode.

"I'll give your parents a call. I'll be right back. Just sit here, ok?" She places a bin next to my feet, in case I have to throw up, I presume.

I don't know how long she is gone or why she even knows whose parents to call. I curl up in a ball, trying to calm my body. My mom can't find me this way. She will never understand, she never does. Be strong, Kaya, be strong.

I feel the darkness creep up on me. I see it all around. I shut my eyes, squeeze them tight. My breathing is too loud, my heartbeat too fast. I feel empty and hollow and so, so alone. This school where I've spent many days, it's become my prison. My life is my prison. I thought I was better. I tried so hard to be better. To open up to Theresa and other doctors. To see the bright side of things, to take one day at a time. But it's all too much. Every day is a day less worth living. The more of something there is, the less worth it is. Maybe life for me is the same. I tried to get out when I still could, and now I am stuck in hell. Or maybe I'm dead already, and in the real world mom and dad and Hailey are mourning me, but slowly starting to move on with their lives. Did my parents tell my friends the real reason I died? Or will they say it was an accident? I guess it kind of was—an accident that they got an insane person as their daughter. And while that is happening in the real world, I'm in hell. Living my worst day, every day. Thinking I'm better, rising high—only to crash so much more violently.

Eventually my mother comes in. I don't know how I get in the car or home or into bed. But here I am. In bed, in the dark. Time is slow and fast, painfully slowly slipping away from me. I'm sure my parents know. They are probably on the phone with a doctor or whatever, describing whatever they have seen of my breakdown.

This is what it boils down to now. A breakdown. I am weak. I can't even act. I've become so pathetic, it's just sad. At least last time around it came as a shock. I was able to smile and laugh and pretend and act. Now I can't even get up.

I turn around and bite my cushion. I scream, gag myself. I want the pain to stop. There is this black fire inside of me, burning everything. Ashes are all that will be left and I can't anymore. I just can't.

Hailey, mom, dad. The three people I care most about. In one day, I've lost and disappointed them all. In movies, this only happens after something terrible occurs and the person does some huge evil stunt. In real life, you don't need anything big. Small things are so much more poisonous. They infiltrate your heart and kill it, slowly murdering the part that cared about the person who did this to you. In all these cases—me, my part in their hearts.

I've fought with Hailey before, but never this bad. Never this honestly. Never this cruelly. And it wasn't even a proper fight. But she can't forgive me, I know it. I can't forgive myself. I never wanted to hurt her and I did. But I did want to hurt her—I did. Because a dark part of me blames her for it all. Or at least she helped. She asked if I was fine, but she never questioned. She could have helped me, forced me. But she didn't.

My parents are the same story, just a different page of the same book. I am their daughter, they must have realized something. Well, apparently not. Apparently, they were too busy with the perfect side of me to realize how broken I am.

Tim pops into my mind. I care about him. A lot. Who am I kidding, he is the reason I held it in for so long. When he came into my life, he was my new sun. I used all my pretense that I normally reserve for the outside world on myself. I convinced myself we're just friends, but we are obviously more. Our jokes, his understanding, our date. Ruby was right—it was coffee. Typical first date material.

I don't know how I summon the strength to do so, but I get up. In the dark I walk to my desk, grab my bag and pull out my phone. Tim, I need him.

Hey! I know it's late, but can we meet for breakfast tomorrow? Need to talk to you.

25

"Sorry, I'm late. Overslept." I smile at Tim, no need to pretend. Even though I had to sneak out of the house, even though my mother's questions drove me crazy last night, even though it is all dark—when I see him, my heart skips a few beats and my insides are suddenly not that hollow.

"No worries. I just got here myself." He hugs me; I feel safe, welcome. I hug him back, holding on a little bit tighter, a little bit longer. His warm smile shows me that I was right to do so. We walk to the line together, talking about this and that. How glad we are that it's weekend, how he has this family thing tonight. It's so easy to talk to him, so simple. My heart is not free and darkness is still there, but he is like this perfect patch of grass that has to be somewhere in the park. Untouched, not yet corrupted, not yet destroyed. We grab a table outside under a sun screen. I love Starbucks breakfasts; an Iced Chai, a muffin, a cute guy.

"So how are you feeling? Hailey said you got ill." And all of a sudden, a flip is switched and darkness is back. The sun is too hot, the muffin to crumbly, the tea too sweet.

"Did she now? Ya, much better. Food poisoning or something." He looks at me and although his blue eyes are hidden behind his shades, he seems concerned.

"I'm fine, really."

"I'm guessing that is the standard phrase, isn't it?" I run my fingers through my hair, shifting uncomfortably. The heat is getting to me. Even though it's already October, I'm warm. Way too warm.

"What do you mean?"

"'I'm fine'. That's how you convince people. I don't believe it." I know what he means; I know he is being observant and all, but I don't need this. Why is he bringing it up? I want to talk about us, not this. Not the darkness. I can't let it win.

"I'm fine, ok? Drop it." His mouth is a hard line, his voice lower and softer.

"You can be honest, don't lie."

"I said I'm fine, ok? Please, let's not talk about it." I try to smile, although I'm gritting my teeth. It's following me; a drop of the darkness and the black and the poison is infiltrating us. It's not much, but then again it never was. It just spreads—like food coloring in a pot of icing. Before you know it, everything is black.

The tension between us is suddenly separating us like an invisible wall. I long to erase it, to tear it down. I need this connection, I need him. Leaning forward, I touch his arm. I push my shades into my hair so he can see my eyes.

"I'm sorry. I just want to enjoy hanging out with you, not let it be poisoned. Forgive me?" He nods slowly, studying me. I hate that I can't see his eyes—I hate that he has that advantage over me.

"Sure." His smile appears like another sun in the sky. I need to tell him, I just can't hide it. I swear people say that good things take time, but really great things happen in the blink of an eye. And that's what it took for me. It was building, this thing between us, but now that it hit me in the face I can't ignore it any longer. It's finally right.

Guess it's true that sometimes you have to run away in order to know who is following. He followed. When even Hailey deserted me, he was there for me. I hurt everyone, lost everyone. Not him. He is the only one who could never be collateral damage. He can heal me, I know it. He is the puzzle piece; the light in my life.

"What are you smiling about?" I shake my head. I'm smiling? That's the effect he has on me. When I thought I'd never laugh again, suddenly I smile. And I don't even try.

"I can't believe we came into each other's lives just when I needed it. I'm glad I have you."

"Ok, glad I have you too. Biology would really suck without you."

"Life would suck without you." His smile wavers for an instant. Maybe he knows what I really mean: that life sucks. And he is the only thing making it better. I hate knowing how it hurts him to know I'm unhappy. I take a deep breath. I need to tell him; I'm at a breaking

point, I know it. I can't do this whole coy dating thing.
I need him now. That's the thing with issues: when you
have them, normal teenage life doesn't really exist that
much anymore.

"Ok, so, I wanted to talk to you."

"I got that from your text." He looks at me smugly
and I can't resist hitting his arm just a little bit. He pretends to be hurt, extracting another smile from me.

"Seriously though. I'm just going to come right out
and say it. I know this is maybe not how 'normal' girls
would do it. I know I should technically be all coy and
shy, but I don't have the energy. It's clear what's going
on between us, and I think we should stop pretending.
Be honest."

"What are you talking about? Kaya, I'm not following." He looks confused. A bad feeling is spreading inside
of me, but I push it away. Not now, please.

"Us. I know you like me and I like you too. So I think
we should just stand up to it; skip the whole dating part."
He mumbles something incoherently and runs his hands
through his hair nervously.

"Wait, are you saying you want to be in a relation-
ship?" I nod excitedly. His face pales ever so slightly.

"Kaya. I like you, no doubt, and I want you to be safe
and I care about you a lot, but I don't like you in that
way. Just as friends."

My heart runs into a wall. I try to swallow, but my
mouth is dry. I feel like I'm running out of oxygen, like

I'm jumping out of an airplane, no parachute in sight. He doesn't like me. I read it wrong. It's too late. More damage. Hailey, my parents, him. Collateral damage all around.

"Oh my god. I'm sorry, I'm such an idiot", I press out. I keep mumbling 'oh my god' to myself, leaning back when he tries to reach out to me.

"I'm so sorry, I had no idea you thought that way. Kaya, please." I don't want to hear it, I can't. I get up and slide my sunglasses onto my nose. Turning around, I try to navigate my way through the labyrinth of tables.

Tears of anger and despair spring to my eyes, clouding my vision, making me stumble. My heart aches and I've never felt so alone. I hear his voice behind me, I even feel his hand on my arm.

"Kaya, please. I'm sorry."

"I'm fine, I have to go, see you Monday." I jerk free, walking away from him, hoping he gets the message. I don't feel him follow, nor do I hear him. I've lost him. I have to get away from here, I have to run away. Not to find out who will follow; it's obvious that no one will. But just to escape, to be free. I'm constricted, gasping for air. Darkness is everywhere, the world is spinning. I wipe at my tears, but they keep flowing. I never cry, not in front of others. The sunglasses hide the worst, but it doesn't make it easier to see. It's all broken, I am broken. I cry, I can't laugh, can't pretend, lost everyone and everything. I just can't do this anymore.

I stumble towards home, trying to get it together. But my attempts are halfhearted because nothing matters anymore. Why would it? I'm all alone. My insides have burnt out. Just ashes left behind. I'm hollow and empty and so, so tired.

I trip and fall, but the sharp pain I should feel when my knees and hands hit the pavement is numbed. Everything is numbed, everything is gone. I can't feel, I can't think. It's just not worth it, it's not worth anything. I'm not worth it, not anymore. Haven't been for a while. Pedestrians ask me if I'm ok, but I just shake my head and keep on running, falling, stumbling.

I don't know how long it takes me to get home or how far I walk. All I know is that it's not far enough. Every wound I thought Tim's presence would help heal tears open deeper than ever before. Knives are slashing at me, cutting deeper and deeper. They leave my heart bleeding and torn into pieces.

It's back. The pain, the despair, the anger and hollowness I was convinced I'd escaped. Now I know it was all just pretense. Just me acting. The darkness is everywhere, surrounding me, no light in sight.

I know the Californian sun is above; I know it used to be my favorite thing to watch the sun rise over the ocean. That was long ago. In my world, the sun hasn't been rising for years.

I was wrong, I wasn't about to reach my breaking point. I did reach it. My world was crumbling around me and I just gave it the final push. It collapsed into heaps of ashes, mirroring my insides. The wall I had built around my heart has come tumbling down, like the walls around Jericho. This is it. The damage is done. I can't anymore.

Epilogue

I storm into the house and head straight for the kitchen. I don't know where my parents are, I don't care. I lock the door. Even if they wanted to, they wouldn't be able to come in. They probably think I am sound asleep upstairs. Let them think that; I can't hurt any more. I don't ever want to hurt them again, I don't want to inflict pain every day. It's over, no more.

Like in a trance, I walk to the drawer, open it and take out the sharpest knife I can find. Its touch is familiar from so many months before. My hand is shaking as I place it on the kitchen counter, steadying myself by holding onto it. This time I'll do it right.

My tear-streaked gaze wanders to the window, but I don't see the garden outside. I don't see the same view that I have seen my whole life whenever I looked out that window. How could I? Memories are part of life, and mine just collapsed.

I'm looking out the window at a lost future and a shattered past. My lost future, my shattered past. People say your life is shown like a movie those few seconds before you're released to another place. It's not true, not last and not this time. All I have is this moment, my thoughts, my feelings. And they are all so painfully numb.

My hand is not shaking anymore. Suddenly, I am calm. I'll be free, finally. I strip off my bangles and firmly grip the knife. A deep breath, no rush. This is it—I'm done; no disappointment, no waking up. I place the blade at the exact same position as I did so many months ago, relishing the feeling of the cold blade against my heated skin. So much has happened, so much has changed. But one thing still stayed the same. I still want the same: escape, relief, the end.

Death is easy, peaceful even. Life is just so much harder.

Acknowledgments

A book is so much more than the words that fill the pages. It's all the time and energy, all the thoughts and emotions that lead to these words being written. All the people that—knowingly or not—contributed to the story and the characters.

Thank you to everyone who worked on this book and helped make it what it is; the cover, the editing, the proof-reading … it couldn't have happened without all of you and I really appreciate it. A special thanks goes to Theda Krohm-Linke who believed in my story. Thanks also to Anne Rüffer—wouldn't have met Theda without you.

I'm also grateful to my family, genetic as well as by choice. The knowledge that you'll always have my back and support me from afar gets me through some rough times. Thank you for just being there.

A gigantic, colorful, incredible thank you goes to all the beautiful ladies with whom I got to share a home for two years—my GIH family. You girls are amazing. You have no idea what you've all done for me, how you've influenced who I've become and where I want to go. You all mean so much to me.

Flavia, Livia, Lara, Munchkin, Salma, Ewurama, Conway and Vicky … I don't know what to say except: Thank you. I trust you know what for.

And, lastly, although it sounds too simple for everything you've done for me and keep doing, and for all the support and love I've received from you: Thank you, Mommy. For everything.

Love,
Andrina

Andrina Vögele Reynolds, born in 1995, grew up in Switzerland. She spent two years in England at a boarding school, Sevenoaks. Coming fall, she will be attending New York University for Liberal Arts. "When Nothing's Right" is her second novel. Writing is her passion, whether it's an article, a poem or a novel.